THE
MIDNIGHT
LIBRARY

—

END GAME

DAMIEN GRAVES

SCHOLASTIC INC.

New York   Toronto   London   Auckland   Sydney
Mexico City   New Delhi   Hong Kong   Buenos Aires

SPECIAL THANKS TO BEN JEAPES
AND ROBIN WASSERMAN

—

ISBN 0-439-87188-3

Series created by Working Partners Ltd.
Text copyright © 2005 by Working Partners Ltd.
Interior illustrations © 2005 by David McDougall

12 11 10 9 8 7 6 5 4 3 2 1   6 7 8 9 10 11/0

Printed in China
First printing, November 2006

Welcome, reader.

My name is Damien Graves,
curator of that secret
institution:

The Midnight Library.

Where is The Midnight Library, you ask?
Why have you never heard of it?
For the sake of your own safety, these questions are better left
unanswered. However . . . as long as you promise not to reveal
where you heard the following (no matter who or *what*
demands it of you), I will reveal what I
keep here in my ancient vaults.
After many years of searching,
I have gathered the most terrifying
collection of stories known to
humanity. They will chill you to
your very core, and make
the flesh creep on your young,
brittle bones. So go ahead, brave
soul. Turn the page. After all, what's
the worst that could happen . . . ?

Damien Graves

LOOKING FOR DAYLIGHT? KEEP DREAMING.
THE MIDNIGHT LIBRARY CONTINUES....

———

VOICES

BLOOD AND SAND

END GAME

THE CAT LADY

LIAR

THE
MIDNIGHT LIBRARY:
VOLUME III

Stories by Ben Jeapes and Robin Wasserman

——

CONTENTS

End Game

The inside of the car was soundproofed, and a glass partition cut off the front seats from the back. The only sound in the rear was Simon's game: the *bleep-bleep-bleep* as he worked the controls, the triumphant tinny fanfare as another dragon bit the dust. He didn't hear the crackle of wheels on gravel as the car swept up the driveway to the house. His eyes were fixed on the small LCD screen of his favorite handheld gaming device. He had been battling at this game for so long, but he still remembered the cheat hint on the Web site: *The warrior must get off his horse* before *he walks through the gate, so that the dragon misses him when it swoops down — but*

1

do it too soon and the bridge crumbles and you fall to your death, so it has to be just right.

The chauffeur opened the door, and a blast of cold air hit him on the side of the face.

"We're home, Master Simon," the man said.

Simon Edwards glared at him, then at the screen, just as the warrior's headless body toppled to the ground. He had been distracted at exactly the wrong moment. The dragon swooped up into the air, the head clutched between its claws and dripping a digital trail of red blobs.

"You're fired!" Simon shouted.

"If you say so, Master Simon," the man replied. "Dinner will be at seven."

Of course, Simon thought as he slouched into the house, he didn't really have the authority to fire anyone. You couldn't do that when you were twelve. But it was a nice thought, being able to control the outside world as well as he could control the one in his computers.

He paused at the front door, and twisted around to look back. The house was set high above the treeline and overlooked the entire town. Down there, Simon realized, there were other people. He bit his lip. His schoolmates were down there. People with lives. People with one another.

It was a lonely thought, but Simon had gotten good at turning the lonely thoughts against themselves. *Yes, they had one another,* he told himself, *but they lived their lives crammed together. Constantly rubbing shoulders. Constantly in one another's way.*

But up here, he was free. He was above all of them, looking down on all of them.

He had tried inviting some of them back to his place, once. His mom had suggested it. She had probably read it in a book on child development: *Encourage your child to make friends.* But none of them had come, even though Simon had described the huge television set, his vast library of games and DVDs. He had even exaggerated a teeny bit—he didn't *really* have a den with flat-screen televisions on every wall showing a dozen different channels all at once. But no, none of them had been interested.

Well, let them stay away, he decided as he turned back

to the house. Simon wouldn't let himself envy them. He had something that was better than anything they had. Something that was, in every sense, better than reality.

Hello, SIMON and welcome to <u>betterthanrealitygames</u> <u>.world.</u> [If you're not SIMON, then click here.]

The words flashed on to the screen as Simon loaded the browser and settled down in front of his computer. He had set <u>betterthanrealitygames.world</u> as his home page, and his house had the fastest broadband connection you could get. He just had to turn on the computer, and there it was.

The glow of the monitor was the only light in Simon's room. The bright reds and greens and yellows washed across his face, and he smiled. The site was more reliable than any friend, warm and inviting, and always there for him.

It had been a typical evening: do homework, play games, eat, play more games. All supervised by Templeton, the butler, and Mrs. Solomon, the housekeeper. Dad was still at the bank and Mom was out doing her charity work. Then, at nine-thirty sharp, bedtime. The servants wouldn't fuss if he stayed up, but his parents might if they happened to come home. They'd remember something they had once heard about bedtimes. Like they were good parents, or something.

But betterthanrealitygames.world was how Simon always ended his day. These games were definitely better than reality — better than anything else in his life, in fact. Games that made you think; games you couldn't just walk through. Games that were never the same twice.

As it always did, his mouse cursor hung over the link for custom-made games. He had gone there once before, but one look at the prices had changed his mind. If only there were a free sample or demo — but no, once you got past the prices, you had to enter your card details. He didn't *have* a credit card and he knew from experience he'd be asking for a world of hurt if he entered Mom's or Dad's. That was one definite way of getting their attention, but it had drawbacks, like having his PC taken away for a week.

He sighed, and there was a knock at the door. It opened a crack, and a woman's head poked around it. She had long brown hair and wide-spaced hazel eyes, just like Simon.

Simon jumped up. "Mom!"

"Hello, darling. Still up?" Mrs. Edwards didn't come into the room. "I haven't seen much of you lately, have I? Go to bed now, and we'll have a nice chat in the morning. Good night!"

The door closed before Simon could even open his mouth.

He turned back to the computer and logged off. *A nice chat in the morning*, he muttered to himself. Sure! Except that by the time he was up, she'd have some new emergency to deal with and she'd have already left for the office. Her charity work looked after crises all around the world. Anything from distressed dolphins to Guatemalan orphans. Anything that wasn't him.

He switched off the monitor, and the room was left in darkness.

Something was shining through Simon's eyelids. He pried them open and peered sleepily across the room.

The monitor was on again, and the familiar bright colors of <u>betterthanrealitygames.world</u> splashed around the room. Simon frowned. He was sure he had turned it off.

He curled up into a ball and pulled the duvet over his head. Somehow the light still got in, and he couldn't get back to sleep. He threw the cover back angrily. He would have to completely shut it down — and this time pull the plug to make sure.

But when he approached the computer, what he saw wasn't the usual welcome screen.

Hello, SIMON. As one of our most valued customers, you qualify for a FREE CUSTOM-MADE GAME. Just fill in the boxes below and your FREE CUSTOM-MADE GAME will be mailed directly to you.

"Free, huh?" Simon muttered. One thing he had learned a long time ago was that no successful company ever gave you something that was *really* free. But he would play along until he discovered what the catch was, then pull out.

So he sat down and placed his hand on the mouse.

First, there was all the demographic stuff: age, gender, occupation — in other words, info that would go straight to the marketing department so that they could spam him forever. He declared himself to be an eighty-year-old widow, employed as a brain surgeon, earning a million dollars a year.

Then came the more important items.

YOUR GAME:
Would you like your game to be tame or dangerous?

Oh, please, Simon thought. He clicked on "dangerous" without even thinking about it.

Would you like your game to be set in your hometown, a generic town, or a fantasy world?

The cursor hovered over *fantasy world.* Set a game in his town? Yeah, right! Simon snorted. His town was . . . but, now that he thought about it, his town was *exactly* the kind of place that could benefit from a little bit of arcade-style action. So he clicked on "hometown."

End Game

Would you like your game to be reality-based, or as real as life?

Simon frowned. What was the difference? Then he thought of those tedious arcade games where you control a skateboarder zooming around a fantasy arena forever; other times, you're an unseen gunman blasting away at criminals and aliens in an endless maze. Those were reality-based, and you instantly got the hang of them, once you realized they were all basically the same thing, over and over. Whereas, if anything could be said for real life, it was that each day could be completely different from the one before. So Simon moved the cursor over *real as life* and clicked.

He awoke with a gasp. Sunlight was streaming through the curtains, and the birds were singing outside. The blank screen of the computer stared impassively at him from across the room.

He frowned at it. Blank screen? He had turned it off before going to bed, but hadn't it come on again, and hadn't he . . . ?

He shook his head to clear it. *Sure, Simon! Your computer offered you a free game! Get real.*

And then he looked at the bedside clock and leaped out of bed with a yell. He had overslept by nearly an hour!

Simon showered, dressed, and threw books in his bag at warp speed. He would have to skip breakfast. The car would take him to school at River Park, but it was as unforgiving as the school bus. The chauffeur always left precisely on the hour, whether Simon was ready or not. In addition to taking Simon to school, the chauffeur also had to pick up Simon's dad from his daily breakfast meeting. If Simon wasn't in the car when it left, he would be in big trouble.

But there was one ritual that he had to go through, however late he was. He switched on the computer to check for messages.

Hello, SIMON. Your custom game has been shipped.

Simon recoiled. So he really had been offered a free game last night! Strange how he didn't remember going to bed again, though. But there was no time to think about it now. He could hear the car pulling up outside. He ran out of the room, leaving it untidy and the bed unmade. The servants would clean up everything while he was gone.

When he came home that evening, the duvet cover was freshly washed and ironed. And lying on it was a brown paper package.

Simon put down his schoolbag and picked up the package. He turned it over in his hands. It was small and square — the size and weight of a DVD box. His name and address were printed in neat, handwritten capitals. There was no return address and no postage, either. *Who was hand-delivering packages to me?* he wondered.

He went out onto the landing. Templeton was crossing the hall, and Simon called down to him.

"When did this arrive?"

The butler looked up in surprise. "When did what arrive, Master Simon?"

Simon held up the package. "This. For me."

Templeton raised his eyebrows. "You had no deliveries that I was aware of, Master Simon."

Simon felt the first stab of suspicion. Could the butler be joking? Simon would have sworn that Templeton had a certificate guaranteeing his lack of a sense of humor.

"Did anyone go into my room today?" he asked.

"The housekeeper made your bed, Master Simon," Templeton answered. "But otherwise no, no one."

Simon went back into his room and looked at the package. It couldn't have just appeared, could it? Someone *must* have left it.

Could someone have gotten up here without being noticed by the staff? Or was it just the housekeeper, playing her own little game?

Hey, get a grip! he told himself. There was no point getting paranoid. What was undeniable was that this package was here, right now.

He pulled off the paper and held up a DVD-ROM in a plastic case. There was no label on the case or the disc — just the word *Simon* written in black, indelible marker. Would the housekeeper leave him a DVD?

It took half a second to decide that no, she wouldn't. She recently had to ask how to shut off a monitor — she wasn't going to be burning discs in her spare time.

Heart pounding, Simon switched on the computer and slid the DVD-ROM into the drive.

The computer whirred into action, and the screen cleared. A message flashed up in white lettering on a black background. It looked like the text on a really old, steam-driven DOS computer.

Welcome to your game, Simon.

So far, so dumb, he thought. He had seen better graphics on a 1980s arcade-imitation game. The message was just basic computer text scrolling across the screen.

The welcome message scrolled up and was replaced by something slightly longer.

You control the actions of a dangerous criminal. The object of the game is to cause as much devastation as possible to the town.

Then came a description of how to use the controls, which he could have figured out in his sleep. It looked as basic as the first screen. Simon yawned as he picked up the joystick that was plugged into the back of his PC.

And then the screen cleared, and he sat bolt upright as an unprecedented vision of reality popped to life.

"Wow!" he breathed. He was looking down the main street in his town. It was like there was a camera there, piping real-time images straight to his PC. Only this technology wasn't jerky like a webcam or black and white like a security camera. His screen was filled with full-color, high-resolution pictures. His viewpoint seemed to be from about fifteen feet up in the air, looking down and along the street.

It was the end-of-day rush hour. The street was thick with traffic, and the sidewalks were crowded. The sounds that filled his room were the sounds of the main street in late afternoon.

The only thing that told him it wasn't actual, live footage was the man standing in the middle of the road with his back to Simon. He just stood there, ignoring the traffic that crawled by on either side. He wore dirty old sneakers, torn jeans, and a T-shirt. You couldn't see his face, just the back of his close-cropped head. Looking at his broad shoulders and thick arms, he was the kind of guy Simon might think about cross-ing the street to avoid.

Simon nudged his joystick and the man moved forward a few paces. Left, and the man turned left. The whole scene shifted with him, so that the man kept his back to the screen. Now he was facing the stores.

No way! Simon thought, *There's no way they could have digitized the whole town in just a few hours!* Because that was when he had placed his order, just a few hours ago. Did they have templates arranged for different towns? Or at least, all the towns in their customer database? But there, on-screen, just to the left, was the church with scaffolding up the front. Simon drove past it every day on the way to school, and he knew the scaf-folding had only gone up two days ago. They must have updated their database pretty fast. Maybe it was all tied in to some kind of satellite feed.

Whatever it was, he decided that he was really going to put this simulation to the test. They went to such efforts to make this seem completely real; it was his duty to try to break it. He set the man running at an easy, gentle lope along the sidewalk. People quickly got out of his way on either side. Sometimes they looked like people Simon knew — the school librarian, someone who worked for his dad — but then they were gone from view as the man continued running.

Using the joystick, Simon turned the man left off the main street and tried the park, the river, then a roundabout route back to the center of town. The man responded instantly to Simon's every command, and there wasn't the slightest hint of load time between scenes. It was as if everything was really happening in town.

The man came to an intersection, and Simon took his hands off the joystick. He had tried sending the man randomly around town; maybe Simon needed some kind of strategy. But what? On screen, the man had obediently stopped and was waiting for Simon's next command.

Suddenly, a message popped up in a box. It was the same old font, black on a gray background.

Remember, BRAINIAC, you are controlling a DANGER-OUS CRIMINAL. So do something DANGEROUS.

"Well, excuse me for living," Simon said. "Got any

suggestions — whoa!" As if in reply, another message had appeared.

Why not BREAK IN somewhere? You can choose:
- *the hospital*
- *the gas company*
- *the bakery*

"The *bakery?*" Simon said scornfully. "Sure, all dangerous criminals break into bakeries."

But he selected the bakery anyway, because he wanted to test the game with the least obvious choice. And while he had nothing against the hospital (he might get sick one day) or the gas company (he had to stay warm), the owner of the bakery on Boyle Street, two blocks away from Simon's school, was another matter. The man was permanently grouchy and seemed to have a personal grudge against all the town's young people. *This*, Simon thought, *could be interesting*.

As soon as he made his choice, the man started to run back through town.

"Hey, come on!" Simon protested. He had assumed

that selecting the bakery option would take the man straight there, like jumping to another scene. But the downside of this game was that everything seemed to happen in real time, which meant that moving more than a short distance seemed to take forever. He pressed forward on the joystick with all his strength, but the man kept running at the same pace. Simon had already gotten used to controlling the man's every move, and it was a strange feeling having to sit back and watch him.

The man turned into the strip mall and jogged past the flower shop and the sporting-goods store, stopping outside the bakery window. And there he stood, not moving. His hands hung by his sides and he stared through the plate glass at the racks of cookies and cakes. His back was still turned to Simon, and his reflection in the glass was too dark for Simon to pick out any features.

"Hello?" Simon called out. "Hell-*oo*? Going anywhere?"

Still the man just stood, until Simon experimentally prodded the joystick and the man took a couple of steps.

"Yes!" Simon shouted in satisfaction. The man was

back under control. Simon made him walk into the store and look around. There were shelves full of loaves of bread, cakes, muffins, and cookies. There was even a glass-topped counter with the cash registers on it. It was exactly as it always looked in real life.

"This is wicked," Simon murmured. He had thought that maybe the game's makers got their designs for the town from satellite images, but what satellite could look into a store?

The owner of the bakery was behind the counter. He was middle-aged, dark-haired, and plump, with a permanently sour expression. Like the inside of the store, he looked just like the real thing.

"May I help you?" the baker asked. Simon's speakers were good enough to make it sound like the man was in the room with him. It was even the same sing-song tone of voice the baker always used. *He only pretends to like the customer,* Simon thought.

"Yeah, I'm going to smash up the place," he said cheerfully to the screen. "But first I'll take all of your money, 'cause I'm a dangerous criminal." He studied the buttons on the side of the joystick. Was there anything to make the man talk? Apparently not. He assumed the man couldn't speak, so Simon just had him walk around the end of the counter toward the register.

"Hey!" The baker stepped forward and poked the man in the chest. "Back off!"

Simon hadn't yet made the man do anything other than run. How could the simulated baker fight back? On an impulse Simon pressed the red button on the joystick — the button he would press if this was a war game and he wanted to fire something. The man on the screen put his hand on the baker's chest and shoved, hard. The baker staggered back and smashed into a glass cabinet as the lifelike sound of shattering glass echoed from the computer's speakers. He cowered in the shards on the floor, staring up at his attacker with a terrified expression.

The man just stood there and stared, because Simon was too stunned to enter any more commands.

"Wow!" he whispered. He was used to combat games, games where improbable superhuman heroes could fling one another around like pillows. But there had been something *real* about this. The way the man had braced himself, the strength of his shove; it looked genuine, like one real flesh-and-blood human had just assaulted another.

Simon came back to his senses with a shudder. *Hey, get a grip,* he told himself. However good the images were, they were all just bytes in a memory card. Nothing more. And he had unfinished business here.

Simon made his man turn toward the register, which opened with a *ka-ching*. The screen image emptied the cash out into his pockets. Just before Simon turned the man to leave, a note popped up on the screen.

Want to cause some more damage? Remember — this is a DANGEROUS CRIMINAL.

More damage? Why not! Simon thought. After all, it was only a game.

The man was standing next to some shelves. Simon pressed the red button again, and the man grabbed the shelves, then heaved. Baked goods cascaded across the floor in clouds of flour. With a little further experimentation, Simon found that keeping his finger pressed on the red button, instead of tapping it, was enough to send the man into *wreck* mode. If the man was standing next to the baker, he hit him; if he was standing next to something breakable, he broke it.

Simon worked his way around the store, smashing more shelves, kicking in the glass counter, pulling down the light fixtures. Then he noticed a door behind the counter. Using the joystick, he steered the man over and wrenched it open. It led into a tile-lined room, lit by fluorescent striplights. Along one wall was a large, stainless-steel baker's oven. The door in the front was metal and glass, and a row of dials and knobs ran along the top. A small message popped up in the top right-hand corner of the screen:

Move cursor over items to get values.

Simon slid the cursor over the oven.

Baking oven. Six months old. Retail value: $10,000.00

Wow, it cost almost as much as his dad's TV!

You can cause some REAL damage in here, Simon!

Simon pressed the red button again, but this time the man just stood there.

Use the chair for maximum damage.

The chair? Simon made the man look around the room. There was a steel-framed chair in one corner, so he moved the man over to it. Further experimentation revealed that the green button made the man pick it up. Then it was back to the red button. The man heaved the chair up with both hands and swung it down hard against the oven. The speakers rattled with an ear-wrenching, metallic boom. On-screen, the oven's dials shattered and some of the knobs snapped off. Simon smashed it again and again, until the chair was just a pile of bent tubing and the oven was dented and battered as if it had been in a train crash.

Shaking and breathing hard as if he was doing the wrecking himself, Simon sent the man into the next room. The baker obviously used this one as an office. The man overturned the desk and kicked the filing cabinets again and again, leaving satisfying, sneaker-shaped dents in each drawer. There was a computer on the desk, so he picked that up and smashed it on the tile floor, and turned the desk over. Finally, he flung the chair through the window.

Dimly, Simon could hear a police siren. He realized it was coming from the computer.

Cops coming. Better scram. You have:
- *Taken $1,400.00*
- *Caused $13,093.00 in damages*

Your score is ***14,493***.

Do you want to:
- *spend the money?*
- *hide the money?*

Simon thought, *What could I get with $1,400.00?* Not much, compared to what he already had in his bedroom. No, he would save up and buy something totally amazing. If there was some sort of virtual store on this game, maybe he could buy the man some body armor or a weapon. Simon decided that he would wait. So he selected *hide the money*!

Immediately, the man began to run again, out of the bakery's back exit. He seemed to know exactly where he was going to stash the money. Like before, now that he had a destination in mind, there was no way to control him — only Simon didn't know where the destination was this time. What if the man was going to hide his winnings in a useless place? There was no way this guy could know the town better than Simon. Shouting angrily, Simon thumped the joystick. But the man kept running and Simon could only watch, frustrated.

On-screen, the man was heading several blocks away from the center of town. Simon wondered where the man was going. Did this guy have a secret base or a hideout?

The man kept running. Simon twiddled his thumbs and mentally composed the feedback he wanted to leave at betterthanrealitygames.world. *The graphics are amazing, the action is incredibly real, but the real-time element STINKS!*

The man had reached the industrial park on the edge of town and showed no signs of stopping. It seemed the game designer had decided that hiding the money meant leaving town altogether. On-screen, the street in front of the man started to curve up. Simon knew that route all too well. It was the street he took every day, to and from school. If he could make the man stop and turn around, the whole town would be spread out below him. But the man kept going, leaving the town farther and farther behind. Did the game's map of town extend all the way to the top of the hill? Was there a digitized mansion at the top with a tiny little Simon sitting in an upstairs room in front of an even tinier computer?

But after the fields, between the town and the top of the hill, were the woods. Once a forest had covered the whole hill. Now there was just a strip of trees near the top, a barrier that cut off Simon's house from the rest of town. The man entered the woods and, for the first time, he left the road. Simon had another chance to marvel at the game's graphics, the way the setting sun beamed golden pillars of light down through the branches.

About one hundred paces into the woods, the man stopped in front of an oak tree with initials carved into the bark. Briefly, Simon wondered who JV and ZD had been. The man knelt down to clear a space in the moss between two roots and put the money into it. Then he covered it up again with moss and left a pine-cone on top as a marker.

Simon glanced at the clock. He jumped. It was half past eight — he had been playing this game for the last four hours! Most of which, he supposed, had been watching the man run around town in real time. Simon was hungry — the house staff must have called him for dinner, but he hadn't heard — and his eyes were dry and aching.

He looked back at the game and bit his lip. He didn't want to leave it now, when he was just getting the hang of it. Problem was, if he sent the man back to town, then Simon would have to sit through another hour of the guy running down the hill.

The screen was growing dark to match the time of day. Simon pressed some more controls to see if there was any way to activate night vision. Apparently not.

The game made his mind up for him. The man

walked back to the road, then turned downhill to head back to town. A message flashed up on-screen.

That's all for today, Simon. Hope it whetted your appetite. See you tomorrow.

The screen went blank and the disc ejected itself, with a whir of gears.

"Wow," Simon breathed.

He slowly put the disc in its case. Then he switched off the PC. This game had some glitches, but at the same time it was the coolest thing he had ever seen. Ever.

Someone slammed into Simon, knocking the breath out of him. He staggered against the wall.

"Hey, watch where you're going, Edwards!"

Reality came flooding back in.

For most of the morning, Simon had been distracted, thinking about the game. Now he was yanked back into his surroundings with a jolt. He was at school, walking down the noisy main hallway between classes.

But even though it was packed with students going in every direction, most people managed not to walk into one another.

The only exception was Matt Frost — tall, fair-haired, good-looking, and utterly detestable. Normally Simon was adept at looking out for Matt, but today he had been too caught up thinking about the game, and what he would do with it tonight.

The two boys backed away from each other — Simon slowly and carefully, Matt with a slouch. Matt grinned and held Simon's gaze just long enough to make Simon look away. Simon turned to his locker and fumbled with the combination, trying to look like that was what he had planned all the time. He knew from experience that if Matt Frost decided to target him, the rest of the day would be unbearable.

But Matt was distracted by a cry from down the hall.

"Hey, Frost! Still coming shopping with us today?" It was Matt's best friend, Tom.

"You're kidding!" Matt said. "Haven't you heard? There's police lines everywhere down there."

"What do you mean?"

Simon was still struggling with his locker combination, but he couldn't help hearing. Half the school couldn't help hearing. He paused and listened.

"Major break-in yesterday at the bakery!" said Matt.

"No way!" replied Tom.

"Yeah, they emptied the register and smashed up the place."

A small crowd was gathering to discuss the attack, and to his surprise, Simon felt his feet carrying him over. He stood on the edge of the crowd. No one seemed to mind. He moved a little closer. A couple of the kids moved aside for him without taking their attention off Matt.

One of the younger boys — heavy-set, slightly pimply, just the type Matt would consider fair game — piped up. "I really hope they get that guy!" he blurted. "It's not right."

Matt just looked at him. No sarcastic comment, no snide insult. "Yeah," he agreed. "It's not right."

That did it. If that kid could be accepted, Simon decided, so could he. He knew the whole bakery thing had to be one massive coincidence, but wouldn't they sit up and take notice if they knew what he had been playing last night!

He laughed a little too loudly, trying to make a joke. "Yeah, that's the last time he tries to short-change me!"

It was like pricking a bubble. The mood in the crowd vanished, and several hostile stares turned toward him. His face started to blaze.

Matt stared at him with contempt. "Another one of your fantasies, dork?" Most of the other boys started to drift off, and Matt turned away from Simon to face Tom. "Meet you at the lake after school, OK? Maybe we can get some guys together."

"Sure, Frosty. Sounds good."

Simon made one last effort. "Yeah. Um, see you there."

Matt turned back to him. "Sorry, Edwards. The lake's a dork-free zone." He and Tom laughed as they walked down the hallway, leaving Simon on his own, with his fists clenched at his sides.

Somehow, Simon got through the rest of the day, but Matt Frost was always on his mind. Simon had been *that close* to being part of the crowd. He had something at home that could wipe the floor with Matt's popularity. If Simon could just find a way to let people know, then *he* would be the one ruling the school.

Tall Matt. Good-looking Matt. Popular Matt. Matt who would be nothing without his car-dealer dad. Frost Senior owned a very upscale dealership — expensive sports cars that cost more than many homes. Matt was always talking about the flashy models his dad got to test-drive, usually with Matt in the passenger seat.

And what use are flashy cars to middle-school kids? Simon thought bitterly. *None of us can drive!* But everyone can play computer games, watch movies — all the things they could do in spades if they bothered to hang around with him.

That Friday afternoon, the end of the school day was like a prison door opening. The playground was packed with kids milling around, waiting for their rides or their buses, or wheeling their bikes around from the racks behind the gym. As usual, the car was waiting for Simon, directly outside the gate. He pulled the door closed, and it cut off nearly all the noise outside; in the backseat he found one of his old GameBoys and switched it on. The car pulled away.

"Good day at school, Master Simon?" the chauffeur asked without looking around.

"All right," Simon grunted. He looked at the GameBoy's small screen and wrinkled his nose. It passed the time, but compared to the game waiting for him back home, it was kids' stuff.

The car headed out of town.

"I expect you'll be studying for exams now, Master Simon," said the chauffeur cheerfully. "Did you get a lot of homework?"

Simon settled farther down into the cushions and ignored him. The GameBoy was better than nothing. He started to play it halfheartedly.

It was a fifteen-minute drive out of town and up the hill to his home. The town receded into the background, and the road headed up the slope into the trees. . . .

The trees!

"Hey!" He sat up suddenly, the GameBoy forgotten. "Stop! Stop here!"

The driver half looked around. "Now, Master

Simon, you know your father insists I take you straight home. . . ."

"Just do it!" Simon shouted. "Or . . . or I'll come back here anyway!" They were just below the treeline, near the top of the hill. It wouldn't take long on his bike.

"All right, let's not get agitated," the chauffeur said mildly. The car slowed down and pulled over.

Simon scrambled out almost before the car stopped moving, but for a moment he just stood and looked at the trees. He wasn't sure he wanted to continue. He had robbed the bakery and roughed up the baker — in a game. And at the same time, something eerily similar had happened in real life. It *had* to be a coincidence.

But suppose it wasn't?

"Want me to come with you, Master Simon?" the chauffeur called, but Simon barely heard him. He started to walk.

Yes, it could certainly be coincidental that the same robbery happened in his game *and* in reality. But . . . surely the real-life thief wouldn't have hidden the stolen money in the same place as Simon's pretend thief? That would be just too much of a coincidence. So Simon

would look under the tree where the computer charac-
ter had buried the money, he would find it wasn't there,
and he would know it was only a game. Easy.

But Simon had to admit that part of him was hoping
it was, impossibly, true. How cool would that be? How
cool would *he* be? Imagine a game that manipulated
reality!

The woods were quiet, nothing but the sound of wind
rustling in the leaves. Simon realized that he was breathing heavily. He recognized the sensation. It was what he
felt when Matt Frost was gunning for him. It was fear.

Was he afraid the money wouldn't be there — or
afraid that it would be? He wasn't sure.

His footsteps crunched in the leaves, and he kept
his eyes peeled for the right tree. The one with the
initials carved into the bark.

And there it was — the same tree! As he spotted JV
and ZD, Simon slowed down, suddenly unwilling to
go any farther. But he forced himself. He knelt down
by the foot of the tree, and he almost screamed when
he saw what was at the base of the trunk.

There was a pinecone nestled neatly on top of some
moss between the roots.

Simon felt as if he was looking down on himself from far away. He brushed the moss aside, and a damp ten-dollar bill rustled against his fingers.

The money had not been wrapped up in anything, and it was grimy from its night in the undergrowth. Simon already knew how much it would be, but he counted it anyway. Twenties and tens and fives and a bunch of coins.

$1,400.00.

Simon sat down heavily on the ground, the money between his feet.

"Oh, my God," he said. "Oh, my God."

Thoughts whirled in his head: *The game is real and I'm a thief, but it was so cool how I controlled a violent criminal. . . . I could be so popular if I could just handle this right. . . . I don't have to hurt anyone, but I already have . . . but that was before I knew. . . . Matt Frost would be so jealous. . . . I just have to work it all out and . . .*

. . . and, basically, I can do anything I want to do.

Simon scooped up the money and climbed back to his feet. He walked back to the car, slowly at first, then with more speed as his thoughts and emotions crystallized into a newfound sense of ambition.

By the time he got to the car, his plan was fully formed.

"Back to town," he said to the chauffeur.

The largest flat-screen monitor Simon could get for $1,400.00 had a thirty-two-inch screen and a silver-and-black finish. It took up most of his desk, with just enough room for the keyboard, mouse, and joystick. He plugged in the last cable and stepped back to admire it. Yes, it looked good. And in a way, it was appropriate. It was like saying thank-you to the computer, which had helped him get the money in the first place.

A cool breeze blew in through the open window. A faint snatch of music reached his ears, and Simon went over to stand by the curtains. It came from the other side of the trees. From the lake, where Matt and Tom and all their friends were hanging out together. While Simon was here — alone — as usual. Suddenly, the new monitor didn't look so great, but he pushed that thought away. He had to stick to the plan that came to him in the woods. It sounded as if they were having a party down there — the kind of party that should be crashed.

"Simon?" said a voice behind him.

He jumped. "Mom!"

Mrs. Edwards came into the room. She smiled at him and Simon made himself smile back, hoping he looked calm. He wasn't surprised that she didn't notice the new monitor, but he didn't mind. This was the first time in days she had done more than put her head around the door.

"Hello, darling. I wonder if you could give me a hand."

"Oh, OK!" Simon said. It was only half past six. Matt and the others would be down at the lake for hours, and if assisting his mom now meant that she wouldn't come back to check on him later, it would be worth it. He wanted to be sure he had total privacy for what he had in mind.

The pile of envelopes was slowly growing beside him, and Simon had lost count of the number of paper cuts on his fingers. He looked sourly at his mother across the table as he took another flyer from her. Fold it once, fold it twice, put it in the envelope. Then another. Fold it once, fold it twice . . . *This* was why she wanted to spend time with him. Not for his conversation. Not for being her son. Just for his cheap labor.

His mother glanced up and smiled. "Thank you so much for this, darling. It really helps the charity when we get the mailing done on time like this."

"Whatever," he muttered. Fold it once, fold it twice . . . "What's it for, anyway?"

"You remember, the Waterfowl Fund?" she said. "We reintroduced —"

"Yeah, yeah," he grunted, cutting her off. It had only been a polite question, and yes, he remembered the fund. The town had once boasted a unique species of waterfowl down by the lake, until it went almost extinct when Simon's parents were children. A couple of years ago, some chicks raised in captivity had been set free in a protected area near the marina, and now the small community was thriving in the wild. Simon's school had raised money to help it; the fact that Simon's mom had been in charge of the project had given Matt Frost more ammunition then ever in his war against Simon.

"Almost done," she said. She held up a sheaf of

computer-printed labels. "Then we just have to put one of these on each of them —"

Simon shot to his feet. "Sorry, Mom. I have homework to do!" He bolted upstairs two at a time before she could protest.

His room was cold. He had never gotten around to closing the window. He shot a final look in the direction of the lake, where he could hear the faint thumping of bass music. Then he pulled the window shut and turned back to the computer.

"What . . . ?"

The screen was glowing softly. He didn't remember turning on the PC before he went downstairs with his mom. The new monitor's screen was still black, but blood-red letters were painting themselves across it with razor-sharp, high-res clarity.

Ready to play?

Simon slowly sat down in front of the screen. Darn right, he was ready to play. In fact, when he thought about it, he was desperate to play.

He typed Y-E-S.

The screen cleared to show the man standing in the middle of the park.

We can go to:
- *the cinema*
- *the*

Simon didn't wait for the options. He knew where he wanted to go. He typed L-A-K-E in capital letters, and pressed RETURN.

OK.

The man on the screen began to run, and Simon picked up the joystick.

He instantly remembered the major drawback of the game. Everything was in real time, and getting from the park to the lake on the edge of town would take forever. He nudged the joystick and tried to change the computer's mind, but it seemed set. Simon groaned and sat back in his chair. All he could do was watch the man run.

Daylight was fading — outside, through the window, and on the computer screen. The streetlights came on, but by the time the man reached the lakeside, it was almost dark. He walked across the empty parking lot. The gate in the wire fence that surrounded the marina was locked. The man pressed his face to the wire. The lights in the clubhouse were out, and dinghies bobbed silently by the docks. A light wind was blowing across the water, whipping it into white-topped ripples.

Simon made the man look around. Where was everyone? He wasn't going to hurt them — he just wanted to join in the party, in a way they would never forget.

It was no good. Even though Simon turned the speakers up to maximum, all he could hear was the wind in the trees and the occasional passing car in the distance. The man had taken so long to get here that the party had packed up. Angrily, Simon pounded the computer desk, causing the monitor to bounce. Why couldn't the stupid man in the stupid game have started at the marina in the first place, before everyone vanished?

They're hiding from you.

End Game

Simon wasn't sure if it came from the computer or if the message just popped up in his mind, but he felt the anger swell up inside him. Hiding? From him? How could they! How dare they!

He got the man to run along the shore, looking from left to right, but there was no sign of anyone else. No music, either. Eventually, Simon made the man run back to the marina, the only place anyone could be hiding. There were lights in the parking lot but nothing in the marina; a dark stillness lurked behind its wire fence.

"Come on!" Simon shouted. "Come and get it!" The man climbed the fence in seconds and dropped down to the other side.

Simon strained his eyes at the screen. It was the same trouble as the end of the game yesterday. It was dark outside, and he could hardly see anything.

"Find them!" he hissed at the man. *"Find them!"*

But the man did nothing, of course, because Simon hadn't moved the joystick.

"I have had it with this stupid game!" Simon yelled at the screen. "Just as you're getting good, you do this! What's the point?"

As if in answer, white text popped up against the dark background of the screen.

What would you like to do:
- *Sulk?*
- *Go to bed with a glass of milk and a kiss from Mommy?*
- *Rampage?*

"Don't get smart with me," Simon muttered. "*Rampage*, eh?" He selected the last option and clicked. The screen stayed black; he couldn't see the man in the dark. After a pause, Simon dimly heard the sound of glass being smashed through the speakers. Then something hard breaking. Then something . . . squawking?

But it was still nighttime, and he still couldn't see anything. Simon turned off the monitor with an angry jab of his finger.

Simon sat in class, almost in a trance, with the blood roaring in his ears. The teacher was talking, but her voice sounded muffled and faraway.

He ran again through the sequence of events last night in his mind. He had selected *Rampage*. But it had been too dark to see anything and he had switched off the monitor. And then it had been morning, and he was getting out of bed (though he didn't remember getting in). And then he had turned on the TV and flicked on the local news channel.

The reporter had been standing on the dock at the lake. The camera panned across the smashed hulls, the fragments of boat that lay slumped in the water. In a grave voice, the reporter had described how some-one had destroyed the dinghies the previous night. Every single boat had been sunk, and the windows of the clubhouse had been smashed in.

But that hadn't been what made Simon scramble for the OFF button on the remote. With an apology for the disturbing images, the reporter panned to the shore. It was strewn with broken branches and tat-tered nests. The white fragments of shattered eggshells had fallen all over the ground like a fine dusting of snow.

The small, protected home for the rare waterfowl had been completely destroyed, the reporter explained somberly. Just months after being saved from extinction by Eleanor Edwards, the waterfowl had lost everything — not just their home, but also their young. The birds had already taken flight, searching for a new place to settle. Wildlife experts feared they would never find one. The camera lingered on the destruction, zooming in on one of the shattered shells, its fragile pieces stuck to the broad end of an oar. Simon pressed the OFF button so hard it left a small indentation in his thumb. But even when the TV shut off, he couldn't wipe the images from his mind.

He hadn't been able to stop himself from wondering: *What would have happened if Matt and the guys had still been at the marina? What would the man have done to them?*

And then he had seen that the computer was on. A blank screen with white text.

You did that.

"I didn't!" he said sharply. "It was *him*."

But don't you control him?

Simon jumped almost halfway across the room. "Of course, I control him!"

Then it's still your fault. . . .

"It was an accident!" he shouted. "I didn't know what *Rampage* was going to mean. It won't happen again. From now on I tell him exactly what to do. Exactly!"

Exactly, Simon murmured to himself again now, sitting in class.

"I beg your pardon, Simon?" the teacher said.

Simon came back with a start, knocking his pencil case to the floor. Pens ricocheted everywhere. The rest of the class, even people that normally left him alone, burst out laughing. But at that moment, it was the least of his worries.

Simon spent most of the day trying to forget about the attack at the marina, and it almost worked.

"Hey, dork!"

Simon groaned. Frost had spotted him when he was halfway out of the door on the way home.

Matt came down the hallway with a malicious grin on his face. He had the usual crowd of hangers-on with him. "Sorry you couldn't make it last night, Edwards, but we're all OK, thanks for asking. We had a great time."

"That's a shame," Simon snarled before his brain could censor his mouth.

Matt's face clouded. "Hey, dork boy, what's your problem? I thought you'd be glad we weren't attacked."

Simon knew perfectly well that they hadn't been in any danger — they had all gone home before the man arrived. The fact that he couldn't tell anyone boiled inside him.

Matt's face cleared as if a great thought had occurred to him. "Of *course*, they were *Mommy's* birds, weren't they?" he exclaimed. "Oh, did Mommy cry when she heard the news?"

Simon took a step toward Matt. "Take that back," he hissed, "or . . ."

Matt scowled. "Or what, dork?" He casually put a hand on Simon's shoulder and started to walk. Simon tried to break free of his grip, but Matt was bigger and stronger and simply shoved him against the wall. Simon glanced helplessly at the circle of Matt's admirers in the background. No one told Matt to cool it. No one did anything to help. Some of them looked a little embarrassed, like they wished they could be somewhere else. Even Matt's best friend, Tom, looked away. But then some of the others started laughing at Simon as he squirmed, trying to break free. Rage burned inside him. He was in charge of the most dangerous man in town, and they were laughing at him.

Matt leaned forward until their faces were close together. There wasn't the slightest sign of humor in his cold eyes. Simon forced himself to meet his gaze and imagined the man smashing in Matt's face. To his surprise, he felt himself smile.

Matt's lip curled. "You really are pathetic, Edwards," he growled. Then he let Simon go with a jerk and walked away. Simon felt the ice grow around his heart as he stalked out to the waiting car.

As soon as Simon got home from school that day, he rushed to his computer. Once again, he didn't need to wait for the game to give him options. He knew exactly where he wanted his digital criminal to go. And Simon knew exactly what he wanted the man to do.

Matt and his friends hung out at the strip mall all afternoon. They joked around, pushing and shoving one another, gorging themselves on junk food. They got thrown out of the CD store for being too noisy. They got thrown out of the sporting goods store for messing around with the eqiupment. Eventually, they ended up in the park, telling dirty jokes and throwing spitballs. And all afternoon, none of them noticed the strange man following behind them, dogging their every step.

Simon wasn't normally a patient person. But this afternoon, he was happy to wait. Every minute he sat in front of the screen, watching Matt through the man's eyes, he felt the rage within him grow. Matt looked so happy and full of himself — and Simon couldn't wait to wipe the smile off Matt's face.

The computer wasn't so patient.

What would you like to do? it asked over and over again.

But Simon kept the man in the same position — just waiting and watching.

Finally, as the sun was setting, the group broke up, each boy going his separate way. Matt set off on foot for his house. Simon made the man follow him. Matt wandered through town, turning off onto a deserted side street. It was probably a shortcut back to his home. And it was perfect.

Now, Simon murmured to himself.

And, as if the computer had heard him, the digital figure quickened his pace. Matt whirled around at the sound of the heavy footsteps, but it was too late. The man rushed him, grabbing his spindly arms and shoving him up against a wall.

"Hey!" Matt cried. "What are you —?"

The man bent down, lifted a large stone, and smashed it against the wall, inches from Matt's head. The look on Matt's face changed quickly from annoyance to terror.

Simon grinned. This was going exactly as he'd hoped. Each move, Simon was pleased to see, was carried out in accordance with each press of a button. The man was still doing as he was told.

Simon was still in control.

"I'll show you a bully," Simon growled, as if Matt could hear him. "I'll show you who's the crybaby now." He pushed the red button on his joystick again and again.

The man punched Matt in the stomach, hard. Letting out a loud *whoosh,* Matt doubled over in pain.

When he lifted his face, there were tears leaking from the corners of his eye.

"Please," Matt begged, his voice thin and wavering. "Please, just leave me alone."

What would you like to do:
- *Smash his face in?*
- *Choke him?*
- *Break his arms?*

I'd like to do all three, Simon thought, smiling to himself. And then he heard Matt choke back a sob, and his fingers paused over the joystick. Suddenly, Simon felt like *he* was the one in the alley, getting pummeled by a frightening stranger. He could almost feel the rough brick scraping against his back and the metallic taste of blood in his mouth. It tasted like fear.

Whatever Matt had done, he didn't deserve this.

Stop, he typed into the computer. He pushed the joystick hard, guiding the man away from Matt.

Are you sure, Simon? the game asked him. *You can cause a lot more damage.*

"I'm sure," Simon said out loud. But he wasn't. A small

part of him wanted to push the red button on the joy-stick just one more time, to make Matt hurt the way Simon had hurt all these years. He wanted to smash everything in sight, starting with Matt's ugly face. . . .

What's wrong with me? he thought.

He was afraid that if he stayed at the computer much longer, he wouldn't be able to stop himself. So he shut everything down.

He lay his head in his hands and took a few deep breaths.

"I'm in control," he said, trying to convince himself. "Everything is under control."

The words sounded good. But they didn't sound true.

———

The next day in school, Simon was afraid to come face-to-face with Matt. He was feeling too guilty about what had happened — or *almost* happened — the night before. He couldn't forget that terrified look on Matt's face. What if it was still there?

By lunchtime, Simon realized that he shouldn't have wasted his energy worrying. Matt was a hero. All day long, kids followed him around the halls, begging for details. And Matt was all too happy to give them away.

"So I told the guy, 'Get outta my face!' and he just ran away."

"Of course, I wasn't scared — *he* was scared, especially when I told him who my dad was."

"Twice my size, but when I hit him, he fell down like a house of cards."

The more Matt lied, the less guilty Simon felt. And as the guilt faded away, the rage returned. What gave Matt the right to pretend he wasn't just a scared little boy? If only the other kids could learn what *really* happened. If only Simon could be the one to tell them.

The final insult came during recess, when he overheard Matt rehashing the story all over again to the usual adoring audience.

"So I just shook my fist at him," Matt was saying, holding up his fist to demonstrate, "and he screamed like a four-year-old girl."

Simon snorted. "Yeah, right." The words popped out before he could stop himself.

"What do you know, dork?" Matt snapped. The crowd turned to face Simon.

There was a long pause. What was he supposed to say now? The truth? Simon almost laughed. As if anyone would ever believe that. Besides, he didn't *want* to tell the truth: If other people knew about his secret, they might want in on the game. And he couldn't risk that. The game gave him too much power.

"I know you couldn't scare a guy like that away," Simon said. *"You* were the one who was scared."

"Yeah, and I suppose you were there?" Matt laughed, and after a moment, a bunch of his lackeys started laughing, too. "I thought I heard someone whimpering behind the trash can."

Simon felt like someone had socked him in the gut. But he forced a smile onto his face. "Of course, I wasn't there," he said in a cold, quiet voice. "But I saw the guy tear apart the marina. So I know what he could have done to you."

"How did you see that?" Matt's friend Tom asked suspiciously, and the lie came as smoothly to Simon's mouth as if it were true.

"I saw it on this really cool Web site," he said. "They give you all the news before the TV stations. They even caught the guy in action."

"Oh, yeah?" Matt sneered. "So why don't you tell us all about it?"

Simon immediately wished he had kept his mouth shut. He hadn't seen anything at the marina. It had all happened in the dark.

"Well, uh . . ." he began.

Matt smiled, snakelike. "Yes?"

"Well, uh, the guy . . . he got . . . um . . ." Simon thought furiously. How would the man have smashed up the boats? The nests had been destroyed with an oar, but what would cause that much damage to the dinghies? Then he remembered the splintered branches. They looked just like the piles of kindling the servants stocked by the fireplace every winter. He'd once watched one of the servants chopping up the wood, with a large, heavy . . . "An ax," he said. The other kids were gaping at him in awe, and he suddenly felt a surge of confidence. "Of course! He got an ax and started smashing up the boats —"

"Policeman on the radio said it was an iron pipe," said Matt. "They found it in the bushes." He was staring hard at Simon.

"I, uh . . ." Simon stammered. "Yeah, I meant a pipe, but hey, that's not important. . . ."

"You saw the pipe? On your Web site?"

"Uh-huh," Simon lied furiously. "It was —"

"How long was it?"

"Hey, cut it out," Tom protested. "Let him tell us."

Simon held out his hands about three feet apart. "About this long, and then —"

"What color was it?"

Simon rolled his eyes. "Gray."

"So it definitely wasn't an ax?"

"No, it wasn't!" Simon shouted.

"Apparently, it *was* an ax," Matt said with satisfaction. "It was a big *red* fire *ax* from the clubhouse. That's what they found in the bushes."

Simon stared at him and felt the crowd's respect draining away.

"B-but . . . the pipe . . ." he said.

"I made up the pipe," Matt told him. "Like you did. Come on, guys. Let's leave him in his own little world. Just stay away from ours, will you, dork?"

Matt and his crew walked away without looking back. And bit by bit, the crowd around Simon dissolved. Some of them looked back — some with hostility, some just offended.

"That's not funny, Simon," one of them muttered.

Ten seconds later, Simon was on his own again, in the middle of the hallway, his face burning. And the friends counter was back to zero.

His face still burned as the car drove him away from school. Matt was the liar; Simon had been telling the truth! How ironic was that? The injustice of it made him want to scream. He had been giving them what they wanted, and *still* they rejected him. They didn't like him if he told the truth. They didn't like him if he lied. They just didn't like him.

When Simon got home, his first instinct was to rush up to his room. He wanted to get back at Matt, at all of them. But something stopped him. It wasn't just the memory of Matt's face, as the man stood over him, waiting to strike.

It was the fact that the memory made Simon smile.

He didn't want to be this kind of person: angry, violent, alone.

That was the problem, he decided. He was all alone in this; it was just him and the game. If only there was someone he could turn to, who could give him some advice. . . .

He caught a glimpse of his mother, sitting at the dining-room table, and stopped. Sure, his parents weren't around much. And yes, they seemed more interested in their bank accounts and their cocktail parties than in their only child. But still, this was his mother. It felt kind of babyish to go crying to Mommy — but he didn't have anywhere else to turn.

"Mom?" he said tentatively, hovering in the doorway.

"What is it?" she asked without looking up from the stack of papers she was flipping through.

"Do you, uh, have a minute to talk?" he asked, hating how weak and shy his voice sounded.

"Of course, of course, except —" She flipped open her Blackberry and began typing furiously.

"Except what?" Simon prompted her after a long pause.

"Oh, you're still here? I'm sorry, Simon, I'm just so busy right now with the charity. After all of the media attention, things are just crazy. . . ."

"I thought the waterfowl were gone now," Simon said sullenly.

"Yes, but there's a rare species of chipmunk living on the edges of the park and —" Her words were cut off by the shrill ringing of her cell phone. She flipped it open and began spitting rapid-fire instructions into the mouthpiece. "I said *linen* napkins," she snapped. "We're not throwing a pizza party. And — yes, that's exactly what I want. What? No, you just tell them that I said so. Of course, the mayor's coming. I'll make sure of it. Yes, because I asked him, too. No, money's no object, just get it done." She snapped the phone shut and went back to her papers.

"Uh, Mom?"

"Later, honey," she said in a distracted voice. "I'm sure the cook will make you an afternoon snack. Ask for some of those mint-carob cookies you like so much."

She was the one who liked mint-carob cookies. They made Simon want to hurl. But all he said was, "Yeah. Whatever." And then he drifted down the hall. He'd been stupid to think he could talk to his mother about anything that mattered. She was just like the rest. She didn't have any use for him. She had better things to do.

Well, so did he. The game was waiting.

Simon didn't want to sit down in front of the computer. He didn't want to switch on the monitor and grab the joystick. But it was like he couldn't stay away.

Matt's laughter kept ringing in his ears. It was all Matt's fault, Simon realized. That's why he was like this. That's why he had to keep fighting the urge to smash and destroy. It's not because he was a bad person. It's just because Matt made his life miserable. Everyone at school did. If they would just stop pushing him around, everything would be fine.

That was it!

Simon had to see Matt and his cronies every day at school. But if there wasn't any school tomorrow . . .

Simon grinned. It was the perfect solution. He'd get to mess up the place as much as he wanted — or, at least, the man would get to do it, while Simon watched. No one would get hurt. So there would be nothing to feel guilty about, right? If he could pull this off, he'd be a hero to every kid in town!

Welcome back, SIMON.

The words flashed up on the screen. They seemed brighter than before, almost as if the game was happy to have him back.

Are you ready for some fun? Where would you like to go?

Pushing on the joystick, he bounced up and down on his chair as the man ran through the town streets. It was maddening to wait. Finally, the man arrived at the large brick building.

This is going to be awesome, Simon mumbled to himself. And then it began.

The man smashed open the front door. After Simon tested out a new sequence of button commands, the man grabbed a bat from the sporting supply closet and uncovered tons of toilet paper in another closet. He swatted one roll after another into the air, causing rapid white streamers to spiral and bounce in every direction.

Normally, Simon *hated* sports-themed games. This was different. *What else might make a good baseball?* Simon wondered.

After about an hour of batting practice, he realized that he didn't even need to use the joystick anymore. The man was unstoppable.

A small part of Simon's mind cringed at the mess he was making; another part soared in triumph.

And that's when he saw them. Matt and his friends were standing just outside a classroom window, aiming spray paint cans at the side of the school. The man saw them, too. He stopped breaking things and instead knelt under the window, listening.

"I'm telling you, we should get out of here," Tom exclaimed. "Something weird is going on in there!"

"That's why we should go in and check it out," Matt argued. The other boys chimed in with some half-hearted "yeah's." They didn't sound too excited about the idea, but Simon knew they'd never have the nerve to cross Matt.

"We should call the cops; that's what we should do," Tom said.

"And tell 'em what?" Matt sneered. "That we came

down here to do some major damage, but someone beat us to it? Great idea, brainiac."

Simon rolled his eyes. Matt was such a jerk, even to his own best friend. How was it possible that Matt was the popular one while Simon spent every day and every night completely alone?

Tom shrugged.

"Great!" Matt said. "Let's go."

The guys disappeared from the window, but Simon knew they were headed to the door of the gym, a few feet away. And the man seemed to know it, too. He picked up his baseball bat and walked slowly down the hall, toward the gym.

Ready for some real fun, Simon?

"No," Simon said firmly. He'd promised himself that he wouldn't hurt anyone. He nudged the joystick in the other direction, back toward the science wing. There were plenty more messes to make.

But the man just kept heading toward the gym. He had broken into that familiar, long-legged run. Simon tried to bring the man to a halt, but the screen figure kept running.

There was no way to control the man with the joystick now! It was like watching a movie — but a movie that Simon knew was real. . . .

The man found Matt and his friends in the boys' locker room. They'd forgotten about investigating and were just horsing around.

"What're you doing here?" Tom asked when he spotted the man. He just looked confused.

But Matt recognized the man instantly. And an expression of horror flashed across his face. "Guys, we better —"

CRACK! The man smashed his bat into a nearby locker and advanced on the boys, backing them into a corner.

Simon pressed furiously on the joystick, hitting all the buttons in any combination he could think of, but the man kept advancing.

"Let's make a run for it," Matt suggested quietly. The other boys shook their heads, too terrified to move. But Matt didn't wait for their approval. Letting out a loud, primal scream, he raced down the aisle of lockers, trying to veer around the man blocking his path.

"Aaaaaaaaaaah —"

At the last moment, the man swung his bat. There was a thud as it slammed into Matt's chest.

A clatter, as Matt flew backward, crashing into one of the lockers and dropping to the floor.

A silence, as Matt's body lay there, quiet and still.

"NO!" shouted Simon, his stomach filled with leaden fear.

He jabbed at the monitor's OFF button with a frightened shout. It had no effect; the picture stayed there. He dropped to his knees and scrabbled about under the desk, groping for the different power cords. His fingers closed around them, and he yanked them from the socket. The computer went silent. He scrambled back to his feet again, banging his head on the bottom of the desk as he straightened up.

Simon slumped back into his chair, trembling. He couldn't take his eyes off the monitor, terrified it might switch on again — even though he was still clutching the plug. Had he stopped the game? Or was it still happening somehow?

He had to know. So he plugged the computer back in. As the screen flickered to life, Simon could make out some reassuring sounds.

Matt moaned softly, rolling onto his side and curling into a ball. Simon breathed a deep sigh of relief. He was OK.

Well, maybe not OK, but alive.

At least, for now.

The man kept advancing. The boys were pressed against the back wall, their eyes wide with fear. Simon felt sick. He'd thought he wanted them to know how he felt, tortured and alone, but he'd never wanted this.

There had to be something he could do. Then it hit him — of course, why hadn't he thought of it before? Simon stabbed his finger into the EJECT button on the DVD drive. The disc popped out into his hand. He brought it down, hard, against the edge of the table. It didn't break. He placed it halfway on the table and leaned on the other half with all his weight. The disc began to bend, then suddenly snapped in two. A shard of jagged plastic cut into his wrist.

Simon leaned on the desk, breathing heavily, his eyes closed. He had destroyed the source of the game. It was over.

But he could still hear heavy footsteps through the computer speakers. He opened his eyes and screamed.

The game was still running!

Suddenly, the footsteps stopped. The man turned away from the boys and stared at something in the opposite direction. It felt like he was gazing directly at Simon.

What do you think you're doing, SIMON?

At least, the game was talking to him again. Maybe he could still regain control.

P-A-U-S-E, he typed.

Pausing the game is not an option.

E-X-I-T, he typed.

End Game

Ending the game is not an option

He tried everything — delete, escape, reboot, any-thing he could think of. But he was out of options.

At least the man had, for some reason, given up on Matt and his friends. He walked out of the locker room and began running again, down the hall, out the double doors, and back toward the street. When he hit the main road, Simon began to wonder if the man was leaving town altogether. Had Simon scared him away?

Then the man stopped — and looked up. The monitor switched to another view. Now Simon was seeing what the man saw. The screen showed the man's gaze moving up — past the stores, the industrial park, the forest, and beyond. All the way up to the grand house that sat on the hill above the town.

Simon's house.

At first the man began to run in that long-legged, familiar manner, taking the road that led out of town. Only now he was running faster and faster, gaining more speed than ever before.

Simon tried once again to log off, but the computer ignored him. He pressed CTRL-ALT-DELETE and nothing happened. He stabbed at the power switch — to no avail. He dropped to his knees and scrabbled under the table for the power cord. He yanked it out of the CPU, then for good measure he yanked the other end out of the wall. The game kept running.

The man was near now.

Simon yelled and ran on to the landing. "He's coming!" he howled down into the hall.

But there was no one to hear him, he realized. His mother was off at yet another charity event, and the servants had gone home for the night. He hadn't seen his father in ages.

Simon sobbed and rushed over to slam his bedroom door. He turned the key and looked around.

The PC was still, impossibly, on.

The game kept playing.

Simon backed against the wall in terror, but he could not tear his eyes away from his PC screen. He watched as the man crashed through his front doors, then walked up the stairs toward his room. The man reached for the door handle, his ragged breath echoing through the speakers. Simon looked over at the real door. The handle was turning. It stopped and there was a pause, and suddenly the wooden panels shook as a heavy weight threw itself against them.

And again.

The panels began to splinter.

Simon's fear and desperation mixed with rage. He stood up, grabbed his desk chair, and hoisted it over his head. Then, with a shrill cry of frustration, he slammed it down into the computer monitor. It toppled onto the floor, its top-of-the-line screen shattering into a pool of broken glass.

Breaking something helped Simon forget his terror and ignore the man on the other side of his bedroom door. So he lifted the chair and brought it down again, hard, this time smashing the keyboard.

The man threw his weight against the door again, and Simon heard a loud crack, as the wooden panels snapped apart and the man burst through.

Tears of terror blurred Simon's vision. His thoughts tumbled through his mind, fast and incoherent: *I am going to die and it's all because of a stupid computer game and I don't want to die and if only I'd never started playing the game in the first place and this is so unfair and. . . .*

He lifted the chair again and the man lunged toward

him. Simon smashed the chair down against the computer again and again, bursting it into a million pieces —

And Simon suddenly realized that he was alone in his bedroom.

The man was gone.

Simon was surprised by how quickly everything went back to normal. After a massive cleanup effort, school reopened within a few weeks. And it was still just as unpleasant as ever. Soon even Matt was back, with a cast on his arm and his ribs taped up. For a while, Simon felt guilty every time he saw Matt. But that didn't last long: The guy was still such a jerk. He was back to his old self within days, pushing Simon around and making life miserable.

At home, the biggest difference was that Simon no longer had the option of escaping into the world of computer games. His parents had been really mad when they found out what he had done to his machine, and Simon couldn't possibly explain himself. Who would have believed the truth? So he told his mother and father it was an accident — which they didn't believe, either.

Nonetheless, they promptly went back to ignoring him like always.

Perhaps the only true change had occurred in Simon himself. Now that his bedroom was no longer a private video-game arcade, he spent more time getting to know Templeton and the rest of the house staff. He even played cards with them on Friday nights.

Much to his surprise, Simon discovered that there was something almost pleasant and calming about life without a computer. In fact, he hadn't even turned on a GameBoy since the last incident.

Then one day, he came home to discover his parents waiting for him.

"What's wrong?" he asked suspiciously. Maybe they'd found out about the computer game, he suddenly thought. Maybe he was finally going to be punished for everything he'd done.

"Nothing's wrong, honey," his mother said, giving him a half smile. "It's just . . ."

"We know it's your birthday tomorrow," his father

cut in brusquely. "But it looks like we're going to have to take a last-minute trip."

"What?" Simon yelped. "But you promised we'd go out to dinner and —" He cut himself off. If his parents didn't want to stick around for his birthday, fine. He didn't need them. He didn't need anyone. Hadn't he proven that already?

"We're sorry, dear, it can't be helped," his mother said. "But we wanted to make it up to you. There's a surprise waiting for you in your room."

A greedy grin on his face, Simon raced up the stairs. He froze when he reached the doorway of his room. There on his desk, with a big red ribbon wrapped around it, was a brand-new computer and a giant flat-screen monitor.

"Hopefully you'll take better care of this one," his father said from behind him.

Simon opened his mouth, then closed it again. He didn't know what to say. Part of him was horrified to have a computer back in his life. But another part of him . . .

"The man in the store said you'd want the fastest one they sold," his mother said.

"And the most expensive!" his father added.

Simon's first thought was to throw it away. All of it.

But how could he throw away the fastest computer in the store?

This time it will be different, he thought. *I will stay in control. Who cares if I play a little bit of Solitaire once in a while? Maybe some Tetris . . .*

He knew it was a bad idea. A *terrible* idea. But it was such an awesome computer, and he had to admit he was kind of curious to see what it could do.

Just an hour a day, he promised himself. *Two hours on weekends.*

The machine booted up fast — lightning-fast. It buzzed and whirred as the monitor flickered to life . . . then off again. Was something defective?

Suddenly, it restarted. By now, Simon could hardly contain himself — until he noticed a startling sight.

It was unplugged.

Simon's panic-stricken face reflected in the monitor as a familiar font appeared on-screen:

Hello, SIMON. Ready to play?

THE OTHER
SISTER

Sparkle Accessories was churning with the usual midsummer crowd. A bouncy mix of Top 40 pop hits played in the background as Catherine Woodfield greeted each customer with a bright smile. It felt as fake as the new gold and silver lipsticks she had spent all morning stacking in the window.

A knot of three girls finally made it to the front of the line.

"Got anything blue?" one of them demanded. They were poking through a pile of hair scrunchies that they had dumped onto the countertop.

"We're out of blue," Catherine apologized. She

pointed out the alternatives. "We have red, green, yellow, orange. . . ."

"Nah . . ." The girl considered. "Anything sort of turquoisey?"

"No, not really, just what's here — red, green . . ."

"How about navy? Or sapphire! Ooh, I really love sapphire. . . ."

A corner of Catherine's mind was already running through everything else she had to do. Take stock of the bracelets counter, move the earrings closer to the front door — Stella, the manager, had read in a retail magazine that customers liked to see the cheaper items first as it was less off-putting — reorganize the handbag display . . .

"No," she said. "Just red or . . ."

The girl turned away and shoved past her friends. "Forget it. Come on, girls. This place is for losers."

Catherine was already smiling at the next customer, while another corner of her mind took half a second to mutter darkly about timewasters. There was no point in thinking about them for too long, or she would spend all day seething.

Sparkle Accessories had a staff of three, including

the manager, and halfway through the summer it was always packed. But Catherine knew how to make each customer feel like the most important customer in the world.

"May I help you?" she said cheerfully. The woman was at least twice the age of their usual clientele, and Catherine wondered if she'd wandered in by mistake.

"At last!" the woman exclaimed. "I've been standing here for ages."

"How may I help, madam?" said Catherine.

"Well, it's not as if everyone has all day to stand around, is it?"

"No, it isn't," Catherine agreed, her smile beginning to ache. "What can I do for you?"

The customer pulled a green scarf from her bag. "It's this scarf," she said. "I bought it a few months ago —"

"Got any belts?" asked a girl of about twelve, pushing past the woman.

"Next to the flip-flops," Catherine replied automatically, pointing.

"Oh, yeah." The girl rushed off, and Catherine turned back to the other customer.

"Just look at this stitching!" she was saying, holding

up the scarf and pointing to the hem. "It's already coming undone!"

Catherine listened to the woman's complaint with a polite smile. She had been doing this job since she was fourteen, two years ago, when she had started as a part-time worker on Saturdays. This summer was the first time she had worked here full-time, before she started her junior year of high school. The last four weeks had given her more practice than she ever thought she'd need in smiling politely, nodding in all the right places, and ignoring everything the customer said.

The woman went on fussily, "And on top of the stitching problem, when I wore this scarf out in the daylight I realized that it's really a kind of lime green but I wanted something closer to jade."

Catherine nodded and smiled.

"And the way it fits around my shoulders doesn't flatter my figure as well as it could. . . ."

Doesn't flatter your figure? This is Sparkle Accessories! For GIRLS! You're trying to wear a scarf for someone half your age! What do you expect?

"So I thought, if you have something in . . ."

I mean, what were you THINKING?

"Is everything all right, Catherine?"

Catherine's heart sank, though the smile never left her face. Stella, the manager, had wafted out of the stockroom and launched into the conversation. Stella liked to power dress in tailored dark suits, with high heels and perfectly coiffed hair, making absolutely no secret of the fact that she intended to manage a department store one day.

"Yes, Stella," Catherine said. "This lady was just returning a scarf. . . ."

"Then I think you should go in the back and choose some alternatives that we can offer Madam instead." Stella beamed at the customer, who nodded. "Something closer to madam's eyes — say, jade?"

The woman smirked, and Catherine thought, *You're only saying that because you heard HER say jade.* "Right away, Stella," she said, stepping away from the counter.

"And when that's done, I'd like you to move the earrings. . . ."

"It's on my to-do list, Stella."

"Well, *to-do* isn't *done*, is it?" Stella replied, as if she were passing on great wisdom. It was probably a catchphrase she had found in a textbook on retail management.

Catherine knew better than to say anything, so she just hurried over to the scarves to pick out anything that was remotely green.

She found three or four and started back to the counter, nearly cannoning into a small girl who was standing right behind her. The girl hadn't seen her — she was slowly turning a revolving carousel of glittery purses, staring at the way the harsh electric light sparkled on the plastic jewels. Catherine wasn't great at guessing children's ages, but she looked small enough to be about six years old, with untidy shoulder-length dirty blonde hair and a bright, padded coat with red and pink patches. It was an unusual pattern, but quite stylish in a bold, retro sort of way. Catherine wondered where the coat came from, and if it came in grown-up sizes.

Then she wondered why anybody would wear a coat like that in the middle of the summer.

"Hello," she said. The girl looked up at her for just a moment, then went back to the carousel. Catherine paused for a moment, thinking hard. Stella didn't like unaccompanied children in the store — they never had any money to spend, and some of them stole stuff. But this girl looked much younger than most of their problem customers, and Catherine figured that at least one parent must be close by. So she squeezed past, hoisting her fake smile into place again, and went back to the counter.

"Oh, well, I don't know," the woman said when Catherine spread the scarves out on the counter. "Are these really *jade?*"

Fortunately, Stella seemed determined to make this sale herself, so she was the one who had to persuade the woman that a particular green scarf would match her eyes. Catherine hovered in the background, wondering if she could leave Stella to deal with the rest of the customers in line and start moving the earrings. She glanced around the store to see if the little girl was still there.

The girl was looking at the display of handbags now, running one finger over a gleaming lilac leather clutch bag. Catherine watched her curiously — the bag was one of the most expensive items in the shop, and she doubted the kid intended to buy it. But she didn't want Stella to barge over and order the girl out of the store, so she kept an eye on her, hoping her parents would appear.

After a couple of minutes, it became clear that the little girl was on her own. Perhaps her parents were in another store. She didn't look like she was going to be a problem. Catherine had had trouble before with kids who had grabbed something that captured their interest and rushed out through the detectors by the door. They'd set off the alarm but run too fast to get caught. But this little girl seemed too young, too shy and quiet, to shoplift something and run.

Finally, the difficult customer departed with a scarf that was as close a match to her eyes as Sparkle Accessories could offer. Stella vanished into the stockroom since Beth, the other full-time sales assistant, had returned from her lunch break to battle with the rest of the line.

"Be with you in a moment, Beth," Catherine promised. She headed over to the little girl, who had reached a display of colorful designer belts and was looking at them wistfully, as if she didn't dare actually reach out and touch them.

Catherine put on her best smile — one that almost felt genuine — and squatted down beside her. "Hi," she said. "Are you looking for anything in particular?"

The girl looked up at her. Her expression was closed and shy, but there seemed to be a smile there, hovering behind her wide brown eyes. Her fingers brushed against one of the belts. "I like these," she murmured so quietly that Catherine had to strain to listen.

"I think they might be a little expensive for you, I'm afraid," Catherine told her gently.

The girl looked crestfallen. "I don't have any money. But . . ." — she leaned closer — ". . . my sister would really like them." She said it as if she were sharing the world's biggest secret. Catherine drew a breath to ask about the sister — was she older or younger? Was she with her mommy and daddy? In fact, *where* were her mommy and daddy? But then she heard Stella calling briskly across the store.

"Catherine! What are you doing over there? Come and help Beth! Efficient staff are busy staff!"

Catherine straightened up. "I'm on my way, Stella."

Stella opened her mouth to say something else, and Catherine saw her lips purse as she spotted the little girl.

"I hope . . ." she began, and Catherine knew she was

about half a second away from being reminded about the policy for unaccompanied children.

"I'm sorry, these are for the paying customers," she muttered, pushing the belts away from the girl's hands. "I think you should go and find your parents." Out of the corner of her eye, she saw Stella nod approvingly and turn away.

The girl held Catherine's gaze for a moment with dark, expressionless eyes, before brushing past her and running out of the store. The belts swung slightly on the display stand, and Catherine felt about an inch tall.

Well, what was I supposed to do? she thought angrily — angry with herself, angry with Stella, even angry with the girl. *She couldn't just hang around, she obviously wasn't going to buy anything, and if she had tried to run off with something, Stella would have blamed me entirely!* She sighed, wondering if it was too late to find a job that didn't involve dealing with the general public — or overambitious managers — and went back to the counter.

Two days later, Catherine pushed her way hurriedly through the automatic doors into the shopping mall.

It was busier than usual for a Monday, packed with people who seemed determined to walk ten times slower than she wanted to. She had overslept, the bus had crawled through heavy traffic into the center of town, and she had about three minutes left before she was officially late for work.

"Excuse me . . . sorry . . . thanks . . ." she murmured breathlessly, pushing and dodging her way to the escalator leading up to the first floor.

"Excuse me . . . ." She tried to squeeze past the person in front of her on the escalator, hoping she could run up, and the man scowled over his shoulder at her.

"What's the big hurry? You do know these stairs move, don't you?" he snapped, and then looked away, stubbornly refusing to let her get past. Catherine gritted her teeth as she was forced to ride the rest of the way up at the same leisurely pace as everyone else.

Suddenly, a flash of red and pink caught her eye. Something in the pattern reminded her of the child she had seen on Saturday. Catherine gazed around, standing on tiptoe to look over the handrail, and then she saw her. The girl was below Catherine, on the ground level, standing by the base of the ornamental fountain.

Catherine thought back to how they had parted —
she had almost chased the girl out of the store, just to
avoid Stella's wrath. She wondered if she should go
down and apologize, since she hadn't liked having to
act that way. She didn't want the little girl to think
Sparkle Accessories was staffed by horrible ogres.

"Hello!" Catherine called as the escalator carried her
behind a pillar. She tried to move back a step on the
escalator, but it was too crowded, and she got a hostile
stare from the woman behind her. She couldn't move
forward, either. And by the time the escalator had
moved past the pillar, the girl was gone.

Catherine hurried off the escalator and leaned down
over the rail, trying to spot the girl on the level below.
The red-and-pink coat was nowhere to be seen.
She shrugged. It had been a good intention, but not
worth worrying about now. And if she didn't get to
the store in the next thirty seconds, she really would
be late.

Tuesday felt like a long day, Wednesday even longer. Summer vacation meant that a lot of kids had time
on their hands, and Catherine could swear that every

one of them came into Sparkle Accessories to run ice-cream-sticky fingers over the scarves and muddle up the bracelet display. By the end of the day, every part of her seemed to ache: her feet from standing behind the counter, her throat from speaking over the hub-bub of teenage girls and loud music, and her head from always having to talk to at least three customers simultaneously. Meanwhile, she was constantly guard-ing against theft and doing whatever was necessary to keep Stella happy. At closing time, she was glad to activate autopilot, blend into the crowd going home, and shuffle along with everyone else toward the near-est exit.

The mall's exit led out onto the main street. Wed-nesday was late-night shopping, so it was dark outside by the time Catherine left. The plate glass of the slid-ing doors looked black and shiny, perfectly reflecting the bright interior of the mall right back at her. It was like there were two Catherines walking briskly toward each other, and she took a critical look at her reflec-tion. Her shoulder-length hair was getting frizzy again, and she didn't like the way her bangs looked uneven from a certain angle. She bared her teeth to check if she had any lipstick on them, then smiled for real when she realized she looked like a grinning chimp.

The smile vanished when she saw the flash of red and pink again; in the reflection, it was almost right behind her. The girl was standing only a few paces away, and their reflected gazes met for a moment.

Catherine stopped abruptly and turned around, and the woman behind bumped right into her.

"Sorry!" Catherine gasped, but she was already ducking her head, trying to see past the woman to find the girl. "I just . . . um . . ."

"It's all right," the woman said in a tone that meant it very clearly wasn't, and she stepped around Catherine and continued walking.

Catherine tried for a moment to head back against the crowd, but she had no idea which direction to go. The girl had been swallowed up in the wave of people leaving the shopping mall, and even though Catherine stood on tiptoe and craned her neck, she couldn't spot the small blonde head or the pink-and-red coat.

Get a grip, girl, she muttered to herself. It really wasn't that important if Sparkle Accessories had lost one small window shopper. She turned back to the doors and let them slide open in front of her, to release her from another day.

"OK, everybody! It's Friday! Here's something to get you in the dancing mood. . . ."

The local radio station was playing merrily in the store when Catherine walked in, and for once it matched her actual mood. Friday at last! OK, so it was the day before Saturday, which was the busiest of the week, but she was still looking forward to the week-end. The atmosphere was always better in the store, and she had a party at her friend Jenny's house to look forward to on Saturday night. And Jenny had a par-ticularly nice older brother named Chad who was almost certainly going to be there. . . .

Catherine's first customer of the day was a rather lost-looking woman about the same age as Catherine's mom. "School's starting in a couple of weeks . . ." she began.

Tell me about it, Catherine thought gloomily. "Alas!" she said brightly, and the woman smiled.

". . . and I'd like to get some sort of back-to-school

gift for my daughter's birthday. She's nearly fourteen, but I have absolutely no idea what to get her. . . ."

"What does she normally take to school?" Catherine asked.

"Well, her bag, of course, but it's getting a little shabby."

"So let's start there!" Catherine said, leading the woman over to the bag section.

With the rest of the store virtually empty, it was a pretty good way to start the day. Catherine enjoyed helping the woman choose not just a new bag but a sparkly pencil case, a lilac hair scrunchie, and a notebook with a glittery, striped cover.

"Oh, and some of those pens!" the woman said.

"Good idea!" For once, Catherine remembered why her job wasn't that bad. The woman paid with her credit card, thanked Catherine over and over, and left with two bulging shopping bags. *Why couldn't Stella ever be around to see the grateful customers?* Catherine wondered.

Suddenly, she got the distinct feeling that she was being watched. She spun around to find the little girl in the red-and-pink coat standing right behind her.

"Oh, hi!" Catherine said. "Long time, no see!" It was

meant as a joke. The girl just looked solemnly up at her.

"So . . ." Catherine thought quickly about what she could say. She didn't want the girl to think she was going to hustle her out again. "I'm Catherine."

The girl stared pointedly at Catherine's name tag. "I'm nine. I can read."

Nine? Catherine was a bit surprised. She had guessed about three years younger than that. The child was certainly small for her age. But nine was still a little young to be out shopping on one's own in Catherine's opinion.

She looked around — inside the store, and through the windows into the mall — trying to find an adult who looked like they might belong to the little girl. There didn't seem to be anyone. "Are you all by yourself?" she asked brightly. "No mommy or daddy?"

The girl picked up a glittery, cat-shaped purse and ran her finger along its spiky plastic whiskers. "It's OK, you don't need to worry about them," she said with a shrug.

"Oh, OK," said Catherine, not sure what else to say.

The girl stared around the store. "Everything in here's so beautiful," she said. "I wish me and my sister could have beautiful things like this. But Mommy won't let us."

"Um . . . is your sister around?" Catherine asked.

"Hey, Cath!"

Catherine jumped, afraid that she was about to get told off for wasting work time. But it wasn't Stella — it was Jenny and Heather, from school.

"There she is!" Heather had spotted Catherine from the doorway, and they homed in on her like heat-seeking missiles.

"Oh, Cath, we need your help! We absolutely have to get something for my party!" Jenny began.

Catherine glanced down at the girl and flinched. The child's wistful expression was gone now, replaced by what looked like anger.

"What do *they* want?" she said.

"Hey, they're my friends!" Catherine protested.

The girl looked up at her with eyes that were cold and hard. "In that case, I suppose you'd better talk to them," she said, her voice thin and icy. Shoving the cat-shaped purse back on to the stand, she walked out of the store before Catherine could say another word, pushing past the two girls coming the other way.

"Who was that weird little kid?" Heather asked, watching the girl's hasty exit.

"She's not weird, Heather," said Catherine, a bit surprised to find herself jumping to the girl's defense. After all, the reaction to Jenny and Heather had definitely been a little offbeat. "I think she's just lonely. She's often hanging around, and I've never seen her parents. . . ."

"Hey, you two! Stop gossiping — this is an emergency!" Jenny told them. But Catherine had seen a customer hovering by the counter.

"Look, guys, I have to go and take care of that girl. Why not look around and see if there's anything you like?" she suggested. Leaving Jenny and Heather examining the stack of gold and silver lipsticks, she hurried over to the register.

"I want to return this hair band," the customer explained. She took out a glittery, lilac-colored hair band and put it on the counter. "I think some of the sequins are loose."

Catherine checked. It was hard to tell, but one or two of the sequins were sewn on less tightly than the others. "Sorry about that," she said. "If you want, I could replace it with another?"

"Thanks," the girl replied. To Catherine's relief, she didn't sound too annoyed. It was a mystery to her, the things customers got hung up about.

It was an easy exchange, old for new, and the girl went away looking perfectly satisfied. Across the store, Jenny and Heather were trying on hats and squealing at how they looked in the mirror. Catherine knew it could take forever before they decided on something. In the meantime, she twisted the faulty hair band in her hands and looked at it thoughtfully.

"*When I'm not with you-u-u . . .*" Catherine sang along to the radio on Monday morning. She stood on tiptoe on a small set of steps, arranging alternating bottles of perfume and nail polish on a shelf in the window. "*. . . then I'm nowher-r-r-re, because you-u-u are the only-y-y-y . . .*" The song had been echoing in her head all weekend, and not just because it was the current number one. It had been playing when Jenny's brother, Chad, had looked at her from across the room at the party — OK, so he'd gone out to meet his friends before she'd had a chance to talk to him, but their eyes had definitely met in a meaningful way, and she hadn't stopped thinking about him since.

"Are your *friends* here?"

Catherine jumped. The girl stood at the foot of the steps, her neck craning up to look at Catherine. Her eyes were cold and hard, and the way she said "friends" made it sound like an insult.

"No. No, they're not." Catherine climbed down from the steps. *This is starting to fall under the heading of "weird,"* she thought, remembering what Heather had said on Friday. The girl sounded as if she was bitterly jealous of Heather and Jenny.

"That bottle isn't straight," said the girl, pointing. Catherine looked up and saw that one of the nail polish bottles was slightly askew.

"Thanks," she said, climbing back up the steps and reaching out to nudge the bottle with the tip of her finger.

"They were here for ages," the girl went on. "I

watched through the window. I saw the lady with the hair band, too."

"Well, good for you," said Catherine. She had had an idea about what to do with the hair band on Friday. But now, with the girl being so hostile, she wasn't sure. On the other hand, this girl might have really strange parents — they were obviously happy to let her wander around town on her own for days on end. It wouldn't take too much effort for Catherine to be friendly. "Look," she said. She climbed down again and reached behind the counter. She held out the lilac hair band. "I kept it for you." She knew it would only be thrown away otherwise.

At once, the girl's expression was transformed. The ice melted from her eyes, and they became deep and soft and warm. A warm, glowing smile spread across her face.

"Oh!" she breathed. She reached out slowly for the band, as if she was afraid it would break, and slowly lifted it from Catherine's fingers. "Oh," she said again. "It's so *beautiful*! Is it really for *me*?"

"Well, sure . . . um, yes." Catherine felt quite

embarrassed, not just because the girl was so grateful but because, really, the gift wasn't all that special. A reject hair band wasn't exactly an Academy Award, though the girl was reacting as if it was.

"It's so lovely!" said the girl. "It's the best present I've *ever* had!" She gazed up with an adoring stare that made Catherine blush. "Thank you so, so much!" Then her face fell. "But I don't have anything to give you."

"That's OK," Catherine said quickly. "You don't have to give me anything." Her heart twisted. Hadn't anyone ever given this child a present just for the fun of it? Did she always assume there'd be a catch — that she would have to give something in return?

Catherine leaned forward as if she was sharing a secret. The girl smiled more widely and drew closer. Catherine lowered her voice. "Look, my manager's going to be back soon and she doesn't like kids hanging around without buying anything. But you're welcome to drop in when she's not around."

The girl smiled again. "OK." She pushed the band into her hair and straightened up proudly with her hair tucked neatly behind her ears. "And I'll wear this all the time!"

She walked away with her head held high.

Catherine remembered something. "I still don't know your name!" she called.

The girl looked back from the door. For a moment she looked wary, as if she was thinking about what to say.

"Susie," she said at last, and disappeared into the mall.

"OK . . . OK . . ." Stella was running around like a demented bumblebee, which was her usual state of mind before a trip to the bank. "Letter? *Letter?* Oh, God, where did I put that letter . . . ?"

"By the register," Catherine told her, not looking up from the box of spiky hair clips that she was sorting. The clips were sharp and kept jabbing her fingers.

"Oh, yes. I'm going to be late. Where's my bag? Where's my *bag?* Oh, thank you, Beth . . . Now, I should be back by two, see you soon . . ." Stella said breathlessly, and she rushed out, her heels tapping loudly against the floor.

Beth and Catherine looked at each other. When the

sound of clicking heels faded, they both let out sighs of relief.

"Thank goodness for that!" Beth exclaimed. "I'll make some coffee." She disappeared into the back room and Catherine continued sorting the clips.

"Beth," she called, "would you mind being here by yourself during lunch?"

"By myself?" Beth reappeared in the doorway. "Got a secret date, Cath?" Then her eyes widened when she saw Catherine turning red. "No way! You do! Who is it? Tell me everything!"

"It's . . ." Catherine shrugged, but she didn't want to say "it's nothing," because it was something. "My friend Jenny called last night, and she wants us to meet for lunch. . . ." She tried to sound casual, but she could hear the rising excitement in her own voice. ". . . and her brother Chad's going to be there, and Jen is sure he's going to ask me out!"

"Oh, Cath!" Beth hugged her. "That's fantastic! Sure, I can cover for you. But you have to tell me every single detail when you come back! Promise?"

"I promise," grinned Catherine, her stomach flipping over with nerves.

Thirty minutes later, she pulled on her coat and grabbed her bag, stopping by the door to check her lip gloss for the twentieth time.

"Good luck!" Beth called, giving her a thumbs-up. Catherine smiled back, too excited to speak. She was about to open the door when she saw Susie looking at her through the glass. The band was on her head, a sparkly lilac stripe against her blonde hair.

But then Susie saw the coat and the bag and her smile faded, changing into a mask of disappointment.

Catherine pulled open the door, and Susie looked up at her. Her face was a blank mask by now. "I really need to talk to you," Susie announced.

"Well, actually . . ." Catherine began, tightening her grip on her bag. She was about to explain that she had a lunch date.

Susie shrugged and turned away. Underneath the hair band, her hair looked dirtier than ever, and there was a greasy stain on the shoulder of her coat. "Whatever," she said.

She sounded so emotionless, so far from caring, that Catherine guessed the girl was used to disappointment. *Too* used to it. *Jenny — and Chad — would be around for other lunches,* she told herself. "But I can cancel," she went on firmly, and instantly the beam was switched back on in Susie's eyes. Catherine pulled out her cell phone. "Just give me a minute . . ."

"So what would you like?" Catherine asked, looking down at her companion. They were in the sandwich place on the ground level. She deliberately hadn't gone to the coffee shop on the top floor in case they bumped into Jenny and Chad. Catherine had told them Stella was making her work through her lunch hour. There was no way she could let them know they'd been stood up for a nine-year-old girl. Right now, every part of Catherine wanted to be on the top floor, having lunch with Jenny and her brother. But Susie had looked so miserable, and she had said she wanted to talk to Catherine, so there must be something important going on.

The little girl seemed to have recovered. "Chocolate milk shake," she said with satisfaction.

"Two chocolate shakes," Catherine said to the woman behind the counter.

"Here you are," said the woman a minute later,

handing over two glasses and a cookie for Susie. She passed Catherine her change and smiled at Susie. "Oh, what a lovely hair band! Did your sister give it to you?"

Catherine looked down at Susie. Their eyes met, and they both dissolved into giggles. They headed for a table without correcting the woman's mistake.

"I always wanted a sister like you," said Susie when they were sitting down.

"Oh, thanks. Wait — don't you have a sister?" Catherine said, puzzled.

The girl shrugged and started crumbling her cookie between her fingers.

"Look, Susie," Catherine tried again. "Who looks after you? Where's your mom? Or your dad?"

The girl smiled faintly and didn't look up from the table. There were more crumbs than cookie now, and she started picking out the chocolate chips, lining them up around the edge of the plate. "I can look after myself, you know," she said.

"I know, but . . ." Catherine said.

Susie's straw gurgled as she finished her milk shake, and she slid off her stool. "That was fun," she said. "Can we do it again tomorrow?"

Catherine sighed. If there was something difficult occurring in the girl's home life — maybe even something perfectly normal, like her mom and dad going through a divorce — then she obviously wasn't ready to talk about it. Maybe she just needed a friend to hang out with, to make her feel wanted. But in the meantime, she had blown a date with Chad for *this*.

"Sure," Catherine said, forcing herself to smile. "Come by the store at the same time. Stella's usually on break by then."

"OK, I'll be there!" Susie flashed Catherine a shy smile before pulling on her red-and-pink coat and vanishing into the crowd.

"Hey! Hello! Over here!" Catherine snapped out of her daydream. The customer was Tori Parker, a girl from Catherine's class who Catherine had never liked. She waved her hands in front of Catherine's face to get her attention.

"Sorry, I was —"

"Never mind what you were doing — this is important," Tori snapped. Catherine bristled and felt her fake smile melting like ice cream under a heat lamp.

"Look, this handbag is just ridiculous. It's too small for my wallet; it's too small for my cell phone; it's —"

"It's a handbag for special occasions," Catherine pointed out. "It's only meant to be decorative."

"But where do I put my phone?" Tori complained. "Look, I want something bigger but *no way* am I paying another cent."

It was almost the end of Catherine's lunch hour, and there was still no sign of Susie. Perhaps something — or someone — was preventing her from turning up. Perhaps one of her parents had finally discovered a sense of responsibility. Or perhaps she had simply forgotten. Catherine tried not to feel hurt. She'd thought she'd formed some sort of bond with the lonely little girl, but maybe it had been a one-way thing. *Where was she?*

"Are you even listening to me?" said Tori. "You are so useless, Cath!"

At that moment, as if summoned by poor customer service, Stella came in. "Ah, Catherine. Is everything all right?"

"Are you the manager?" Tori demanded. "Maybe you can help." She pushed the offending handbag along the counter toward Stella.

Catherine had had enough. She was starving, and it had just occurred to her that maybe Susie had gotten confused. She might have thought they would meet at the sandwich place, like before, not in the store. She might be waiting there now, wondering where Catherine was, thinking she'd been forgotten. . . .

"I'll be back in a bit, Stella," Catherine said, reaching under the counter for her bag.

Stella stared at her in amazement. "Catherine, your lunch hour is twelve-thirty to one-thirty, and it is now" — she checked her watch — "one thirty-seven. So you are not going anywhere."

"But Beth said she'd cover for me!" Catherine hadn't had the nerve to tell Beth what had really happened the day before, so she had said Chad had cancelled at the last minute — but wanted to see her today instead. Beth had been quite happy to stand in.

Stella folded her hands, and Tori grinned smugly behind her.

"Beth can stand in for you during your *approved* lunch break," Stella lectured, "but not while you just slack off."

Slack off! Catherine wanted to shout. *I work like a*

slave here and I never complain, and now you say I'm slacking off?

"Look, it's just for a couple of minutes!" she insisted. "I've worked all through my lunch break, so you owe me a little . . ."

"Well, you should have *taken* your lunch break. I'm not a slave driver, Catherine. I just have certain expectations. Now, put down your bag and get back to work. It's sure to get busy once everyone's finished *their* lunch."

Catherine wavered and almost gave in. But the thought of Susie waiting hopefully for her was just too much. She would probably stay at the sandwich place until closing time, convinced that Catherine would turn up at any minute. She'd obviously been let down so many times in her life already; there was no way Catherine was adding to the list of disappointments.

"Just a couple of minutes," she said, heading for the door.

"*Catherine!*" Stella's voice was sharp behind her. "If you leave now, I will have no choice but to fire you."

Catherine hesitated, but the image of Susie, alone and disappointed, filled her thoughts. She grabbed her jacket and walked out of the shop. Stella wouldn't really fire her. It was the middle of summer, the store's busiest time. Where else would she find someone willing to put up with her on short notice?

When Catherine reached the sandwich place, there was no sign of Susie. Catherine swore under her breath and went back to the store and found Stella really had fired her.

Hi, Cath!!! Spain is so cool!!!! Boyz everywhere!!!! Heather's dad wants us to see a museum but tonight is CLUB NIGHT!!!!!!!!!!!! Love, Jen & Heather

"Are they having a nice time in Spain?" Catherine's mom asked as she poured a glass of orange juice. It was a week since Catherine had been fired. Normally, she would have been in the store for nearly an hour by now, and would be thinking about the first coffee-and-doughnut break of the morning.

"Hard to say," Catherine muttered. She dropped the postcard on the table and sipped her juice. Jenny and Heather had invited her on the trip months ago, when Heather's parents booked the rooms. But Catherine had turned it down because she'd just landed the job at Sparkle Accessories. She *thought* she would be working all summer.

"Well, no use moping, dear," said her mom. "Maybe you should find some other friends to hang around with."

"I have other friends," Catherine snapped, though off the top of her head she couldn't think of any that she particularly wanted to see. Maybe she had been working too hard at Sparkle Accessories. The only other person she had seen much of recently was . . .

"I met this girl called Susie," she said, carefully not mentioning the girl's age.

"Well, that's nice! Why don't you invite her over?"

"Um . . ." This hadn't occurred to Catherine before, mainly because she tended not to hang out with nine-year-olds at home. And anyway, she still didn't know where Susie lived. "I can't. I don't have her number."

"Not that great a friend, I guess," her mom replied, briskly wiping the table with a damp rag. She had finished breakfast an hour ago.

Catherine fiddled with her piece of toast and kept

quiet. She didn't want to get into a big conversation about her new friend. She'd never been able to lie convincingly to her parents, and she'd only end up giving her mom the impression she'd been hanging around in a kindergarten during her lunch hour.

In short, it was best not to think of Susie at all. Or Stella. Or being broke. Soon Catherine, Jenny, and Heather would be back at high school, and she probably wouldn't even remember this depressing summer at all.

"You need to get out more," her mom said decisively. "Have you done your summer reading for school yet? Why don't you hit the bookstore? Don't worry, I'll lend you the money."

Catherine dropped her uneaten toast back on to the plate and pushed back her chair. Why not? It wasn't like she had anything better to do. "Thanks, Mom."

It seemed odd to find the shopping mall hadn't changed a bit. Catherine had to remind herself it had only been a week. She joined the crowd on the escalator — for once, more than happy to stand still and let the stairs do the work — and admitted that her mom had a good idea. The busy, upbeat atmosphere was already making her feel better, and it was nice to be here as a customer, not a worker.

She glanced at Sparkle Accessories as the escalator carried her up to the second floor. Maybe she wouldn't go back just yet. Fortunately, the bookstore was on the upper level, and she was pretty confident she wouldn't bump into Stella in there. The only books she read were delivered by FedEx and had titles like *How to Succeed in Retail Management* and *Take Your Shop to the Top: A Store-Fire Way to Win!*

Catherine stopped and browsed the display in the bookstore window. There was a three-for-two offer on her favorite series. She was just calculating if the money her mom had lent her would stretch that far when something made her look up. There it was again — a flash of red and pink in the crowd reflected in the glass. For just a moment, Catherine saw Susie, standing not far off and watching her silently. She stiffened, then closed her eyes and groaned.

"Go away," she murmured. "Just go away. You've gotten me into enough trouble." When she opened her eyes, Susie wasn't there anymore. She smiled, trying not to feel like she'd been overreacting. It probably hadn't been Susie at all. That couldn't be the only red-and-pink coat in the world. She just had Susie on her mind still.

"Catherine!"

Someone grabbed her hand, and Catherine just managed not to shriek. As if last week hadn't happened, Susie was clinging to the end of her arm, trying to pull her away.

"Catherine, you've got to come!" she gasped before Catherine could say anything. Her voice was high and urgent and her eyes were red, as if she had been crying. She tugged again, practically hopping with impatience. "Now!"

"Susie, I . . ." Catherine trailed off helplessly. "Where have you been?"

"*Please!*" Susie begged. "You have to come! You have to come and help Laura."

"Laura?" Catherine echoed. "Who's Laura?" Something in Susie's tone told her this wasn't a childish game. And now that she looked more closely, Susie looked even less cared for than before. The lilac hair band was still firmly in place, but her blonde hair hung in lank, greasy rats' tails. And — Catherine's eyes narrowed when she saw it — there was a crusted stain of something red on the front of her coat. Was it . . . ?

"She's my sister! *Please!* She . . . I can't . . . I've got to . . ." Distress was making her stumble over her words and she broke off, putting her hands up to her face.

Catherine made up her mind. Susie clearly needed her help, and whatever it was, it was urgent. Her mind flooded with images of domestic accidents, the kind that happened to unsupervised children — saucepans of boiling water, heavy furniture toppling over. . . .

"OK," Catherine said, turning away from the store and taking Susie's small, sticky hand. "Lead the way." They hurried toward the escalator. "Where is Laura?"

"She's in real trouble," Susie sobbed.

"Yes, but *where* . . ."

"*Real* trouble."

Catherine gave up. Susie was too upset to talk sensibly. Catherine just needed to give the girl time. She would find everything out soon enough.

Catherine shivered slightly as they half walked, half ran across the parking lot. It was a cool day for August. She still didn't know where Susie lived; she had no idea how long this journey was going to take, or even if they were going to run all the way.

"I really missed you," Susie said. Her voice trembled. "Where did you go?"

"Where did I . . . ?" Catherine was so astonished that she slowed down for a moment. She sped up again when Susie tugged at her hand. "I had to stop working at the store," she said eventually. Susie wouldn't understand about being fired, and Catherine didn't intend to make her feel like she was in any way to blame.

They ran through the center of town, dodging the too-slow pedestrians and darting across streets, perilously close to speeding traffic. Catherine realized they were heading toward the opposite side of town from where she lived. They'd gone at least a mile, but Susie hardly seemed to notice. She didn't even seem to be breathing hard. *She must be really worried about Laura,* Catherine thought. They finally reached the local park and hurried down a path that eventually tunneled under a railway overpass.

"Where are your parents?" Catherine panted as they emerged on the other side. "Do they know that Laura's in trouble?" They were on a street she didn't know, with rows of old, compact houses on either side.

"They're never at home — well, not anymore," Susie said. Somehow this didn't surprise Catherine at all.

"Look," she insisted, "you still haven't told me what's wrong with your sister. . . ."

Susie's eyes filled with tears again. "She's in real trouble!" she wailed.

"Yes," Catherine said, starting to feel frustrated, "but . . . and, look, you haven't told me about your mom or dad. . . ."

Susie stopped dead. "We're here," she said, her voice very calm.

They were on the corner of two blocks. A gravel driveway led up to a tall, three-story house of slightly decaying red brick, set back from the street. The large garden was surrounded with bushes and trees, and the roof was steeply pitched, with ornate gables at either end.

"Wow," Catherine breathed, forgetting for a moment why they had come. "You live here?"

Susie was already running up the driveway, her feet

crunching on the gravel. She glanced back. "Come *on!*" Her voice quavered, like she was on the verge of tears. Yet she had seemed perfectly composed a moment ago. Catherine frowned to herself. Susie really did have the most up-and-down emotions she had ever known, even for a child. Catherine hurried after the little girl.

A flight of shallow stone steps led up to a front door decorated with stained glass.

"We have to go around the back," said Susie, and she disappeared along a narrow path around the corner. Catherine looked up at the house slightly nervously as she followed the sound of the girl's rapid footsteps. All the windows were blank and grimy, giving away no clues as to what might be inside. The garden looked so overgrown and neglected that it was hard to believe anyone lived here at all, certainly not Susie's parents. Catherine felt her heart begin to thud. She couldn't get rid of the feeling that she was about to get thrown out for trespassing. Was this really where Susie lived?

The kitchen door at the back of the house was plain wood, painted green. It was already ajar, and Susie slipped inside without looking back.

Catherine hesitated on the threshold. She couldn't

just walk into someone else's house. "H-hello?" she called. "My name's Catherine. I'm with Susie. . . ." She put her hand on the door, and it swung open. She took a breath — *This is it! I am now officially an intruder!* — then took another deep breath and walked inside. "Hello?" she called again. Then she stopped dead.

"Oh . . . my . . ."

The kitchen was filthy. Dirty pots and pans were piled in the sink, crusty with old food and half submerged in scummy gray water. The tiled floor was covered with muddy footprints, and there was a distinctly rotten smell in the air, as if no one had taken out the trash in several weeks. A small pile of peanut butter-and-jelly sandwiches sat on a plate on the table with a large kitchen knife next to them. One of the sandwiches had small bite marks in it.

"Is the whole house like this?" Catherine asked in horror. She had assumed Susie's parents were too busy to look after her. But *this* bad? This much neglect? No, she hadn't expected this.

"Laura's this way," Susie said. She stood in the far doorway and beckoned. Catherine bit her lip. All of this was clearly way over her head. Supposing the parents came home? Could she handle them? Would they get violent? She could imagine the headlines on the news: POLICE ARE LOOKING FOR SIXTEEN-YEAR-OLD CATHERINE WOODFIELD WHO HAS NOT BEEN SEEN SINCE YESTERDAY. . . .

Susie's bottom lip began to quiver. "Please, Catherine, hurry!"

Feeling a bit unreal, as if she were in a movie, Catherine walked forward. She passed a pile of laundry lying in a basket. It was damp and smelled of mildew. The house was surprisingly cold, even though it was summer.

Susie led her down a short passageway into the hall. Daylight shone through large windows on either side of the front door. It had clearly once been very grand; now it was just shabby. Not as bad as the kitchen, but when Catherine ran her finger along the top of the hall table, she left a clear track through the layer of dust. The hallway was lined with wooden panels that made her footsteps echo on the tiled floor, loud as heartbeats. Catherine felt the house looming around her, the windows' eyes watching her every move, the staircase a gaping throat ready to swallow her up.

Susie stopped by a door set into the wall under the stairs. She rested her hand against the wood.

"Laura's in here," she whispered, her eyes huge. "They locked her in."

"Under the stairs?" Catherine couldn't believe it. Or maybe, having seen the kitchen, she could.

"This door goes down to the cellar," Susie explained earnestly, as if that somehow wasn't as bad as being locked in a closet. A fat tear rolled down her cheek. "Mommy says Laura is evil and can't be allowed out. Otherwise she'll hurt people."

"*Evil!?*" Catherine choked. She felt hot and cold all at once, and suddenly the feeling of unreality vanished and she knew she was truly here, right now. Surrounded by some nameless horror that made her breath feel tight and her skin clammy . . .

"Laura's my twin. Mommy and Daddy hate her because she didn't do a good job cleaning the bathroom." Susie began to cry, her small frame shaking with sobs. "But she's not evil, and . . . and . . . I was supposed to clean the kitchen, and I haven't, and they'll say I'm evil, too, and they'll be back soon, and . . ."

There was evil here, sure enough. Or at least, there

would be evil returning soon, when the parents came back. . . .

"Mommy hid the key and I don't know where," Susie mumbled. "I tried to get Laura out, but I couldn't open the door on my own!"

"OK, OK." Catherine gently pushed Susie away, then pressed her face to the cool wood of the cellar door. She raised her voice. "Hello! Laura! Can you hear me?"

There was a long silence. All Catherine could hear was the blood pounding in her own head. The large house was silent — but somehow alive and watching her, waiting for her to do something.

Catherine called again. There was still no answer, but then, on the cusp of hearing, she could make out the faintest scratch. Was it someone moving around?

"I've got Susie here," she called, "and we're going to open the door. OK?"

She stepped back and studied the door. It looked solid. The keyhole was set below the doorknob; they both seemed to be part of the same mechanism, set into a metal plate. The plate was screwed into the door.

"Susie, do you know if there's a screwdriver

anywhere?" she said. She was feeling more clearheaded now that she was actually doing something. It was just an empty house, no reason to be spooked.

Susie blinked at her, red-eyed. "I think there's one in the kitchen," she said. She led Catherine back the way they had come and opened a drawer in one of the kitchen cabinets. It was obviously the tool drawer: Catherine spotted a hammer and a pair of pliers and some fuses and an empty jam jar full of nails and, yes, a good, solid screwdriver. She took it out, gripping it tightly in her hand.

They went back into the hall, and Catherine knelt down by the door. She wanted to keep talking to the little girl locked inside, letting her know that she wasn't on her own anymore, that she would soon be safe.

"OK, Laura," she called. "I'm unscrewing the lock now."

The screws had been in the wood a long time and had been painted over. Catherine had to gouge the dry, sticky paint out of the groove in each screw to get any kind of purchase. Her hands felt clammy on the screwdriver, and she let go to wipe each one on her jeans. Out of the corner of her eye, she could see Susie hovering nearby, hopping from foot to foot.

Catherine tried again. She suddenly gasped as the tip of the screwdriver slipped out with a jerk, leaving scratch marks on the door. She gritted her teeth and started again. This time the tip stayed put and the screw shifted. Catherine quickly pulled it out of the wood and gave it to Susie to hold. Then she turned her attention to the next one.

There were four screws in all. Susie watched in silence while she removed each one. Then she jammed the screwdriver between the metal plate and the wood panel — and heaved. The plate pulled slowly away from the door and left the lock mechanism exposed. Catherine had to unscrew that, too, but it took only a minute. She levered it free, and it fell to the floor with a metallic thud.

Catherine looked at the door and forced herself to take a deep breath. Laura could be just inches away on the other side. What exactly was she going to find when it opened? She really, *really* didn't want to go any farther.

But Susie needed her, not to mention Laura, so Catherine smiled bravely at the little girl. "Almost there. Everything's going to be OK."

She gave the door a push, and it swung open on well-oiled hinges. Catherine leaned in. She could just make out the first couple of steps in a flight of wooden stairs leading down into the dark cellar.

"Hello?" she called softly. "Laura? Don't be scared. I'm a friend of Susie's."

She held her breath and waited for the tiny scratching sound she had heard before. There was still no answer, but she could definitely hear the sound of someone moving around.

"She won't come out unless you go to her," said Susie, and Catherine jumped. The little girl was standing right next to her, so close she could feel Susie's breath on her arm. "She thinks our mom sent you."

Catherine raised her eyebrows doubtfully, but Susie nodded. "I know, because I'm her twin," she explained.

Catherine looked around for a light switch but couldn't see one.

"It's at the bottom of the stairs," Susie said.

"Oh, great." Catherine looked into the darkness. Well, she had come this far. She couldn't leave now.

"OK, Laura, I'm coming down," she called, and started to pick her way down the rickety wooden steps.

The air smelled dusty and damp. The steps creaked under her, but when she paused, she thought she could hear whimpering, which spurred her on. When she felt hard stone under her sneakers, she knew she'd reached the bottom of the stairs. She fumbled for the light switch on the wall and her fingers found it, but when she flicked it on, nothing happened. The light from the upstairs hallway did reveal a small box of matches and the stub of a candle on a shelf next to the switch. Catherine managed to light the candle on the third try, and a quivering triangle of yellow light stretched into the cellar.

The room was bare and empty, with walls that had once been painted white but now were covered with grime. At the far side, half engulfed in shadow, stood a little girl. Her clothes were tattered, her hair was matted and dirty, but her face was identical to Susie's. She was staring at Catherine with wide-eyed horror.

"Hello . . . Laura?" Catherine put all the warmth and encouragement she could into her voice. She took a step forward toward the other sister, and Laura immediately took a step back. Catherine stopped moving.

"It's OK," she soothed. "I'm a friend of Susie's. I've come to get you out."

Laura's chest started to heave. Her mouth moved, but Catherine couldn't make out the words.

And then — a cold, panicky sensation reached out with icy fingers and gripped Catherine by the throat. Just beyond Laura, half hidden in the shadows on the floor, were two long, lumpy shapes. They looked like adults, sleeping. Except how could they still be asleep, after all the noise she'd made breaking into the cellar? Perhaps they were sick. Or perhaps . . . someone had knocked them unconscious.

She had to get Laura out of here. Fast.

"Look," Catherine said. "Susie's waiting upstairs. We can go up together and —"

Her eyes so huge that they seemed to swallow her whole face, Laura slowly raised one hand. Catherine stared in horror when she saw what was in it. An old-fashioned dead-bolt key. The sort that would fit the cellar door.

"Is that the key?" Then Catherine frowned. "If *you* have the key, then why . . . ?" her voice trailed off as she realized Laura wasn't listening. She was staring at something just behind her. Catherine turned to see what it was.

Susie stood on the step just above her. Her face was a stone mask of hatred, and she had her hand clenched tightly around something Catherine couldn't make out. Then Susie lifted her hand, and Catherine saw a suspicious glint of silver. She drew in a sharp breath. The past few weeks suddenly made terrible sense.

"Thanks for everything, Catherine," Susie whispered, taking a step down into the cellar.

"I thought I was safe down here!" Laura screamed, causing Catherine to wince as her voice bounced from wall to wall.

When Laura spoke again, it was in a quiet, calm voice that chilled Catherine to her core. It was the thin, helpless voice of someone who'd given up:

"Why? Why did you let her in?"

IS ANYBODY THERE?

Posters of the missing boy hung in a row at the back of the stage. Luke Benton was pleasant looking, blond, with a smattering of freckles. He wore a slightly bashful smile, as if he couldn't quite believe he was being photographed. The picture that had been used for the posters was Luke's last school photo, taken the day he vanished. He had been wearing his nicest blazer and tie, and, though you couldn't see them in the picture, new black sneakers with a silver trim. His entire outfit had been immortalized by the "last seen wearing" description on all the "Missing" posters that had been plastered around town.

Someone opened the door to the auditorium, and the posters rustled in the breeze. Juliet Somerville made a mental note to secure them at all four corners after the rehearsal. Luke's memorial service was going to be in two days' time, and having the posters waving around at the back of the stage would be distracting to everyone in the auditorium.

Juliet figured it would be quicker to do it herself than to mention it to Miss Worth. Their principal could take the simplest idea and overcomplicate it. She had already turned the rehearsal for the memorial service into a three-ring circus.

Privately, Juliet found it tasteless. Luke hadn't been seen for over a year. His phone hadn't been used, and no money had been taken out of his bank account. He had to be gone forever. He should be remembered in a church service or something, not a performance where people got stage fright and fretted about how they would look under the lights.

Miss Worth clapped her hands above the chatter in the auditorium until she had everyone's attention. "Now, light desk — *light desk!* — thank you . . . and sound desk . . . both ready? Good. Now, can everyone who is going to read a tribute to Luke form a line on the left side of the stage . . . no, the *left* side . . . in alphabetical order of first name . . . or should that be order of age? Hmmm . . ."

Juliet nudged her best friend, Christine. "How about order of shoe size?" she whispered.

But Christine wasn't in a mood for jokes. "Julie, I think Mark just looked at me!" she hissed. She stared across the auditorium. "Look! He just did it again!"

Juliet followed her gaze, trying not to let her doubt show on her face. Mark Logan and his best friend, Daniel Gardner, were sitting together at the back of the auditorium. Mark had a stocky, powerful frame; Daniel was taller and darker, with floppy bangs. Like most of the boys, they were in their football uniforms. All Luke's teammates were going to wear their gear for the service as part of their tribute. If Mark had been looking at Christine, he wasn't now. He and Dan had their heads bowed together, deep in some private conversation.

"I wonder what they're talking about," Christine breathed. "I bet it's about Luke. Mark is such a deep thinker. He's so intellectual. I bet he'll be sharing his thoughts about how loss and bereavement should make us appreciate the finer things of life — and draw us closer together in love."

Juliet shot her friend a quick glance to check if she was being serious. Unfortunately, she was. "No doubt," she agreed. "Or, he scored a really cool touchdown one time and he's telling Daniel all about it."

Christine scowled. "You are such a cynic! You know they were Luke's closest friends."

"So why didn't they volunteer to read tributes?" Juliet asked.

"Oh, Julie, you don't measure friendship like that! Think about it. I mean, losing your best friend overnight — never even finding a trace, just *losing* him — what must that be like? Of course, they don't want to stand up in front of everyone. They probably haven't even begun to deal with what happened to Luke."

"They could have gotten help, I don't know, some sort of counseling," Juliet pointed out. She wasn't sure why; perhaps she just wanted to be stubborn in an attempt to puncture Christine's inflated view of Mark. In the weeks after the disappearance, the school had been overrun with well-meaning professionals urging Luke's fellow students to put their emotions into words.

"And why should they? Why should they talk to some stranger about their innermost feelings?" Christine's voice grew warm. "They need someone who knows them, knows exactly what they're going through."

In other words, Juliet thought, *they should talk to you!* But she didn't say it out loud. It would be mean — and maybe Christine could help the boys after all. As the first anniversary of Luke's disappearance drew nearer, Mark and Daniel had become more and more withdrawn. If anyone approached them, even just brushed against them in the hallway, they could be snappish and irritable. So if Christine was able to help — well, good for her. She certainly couldn't do any harm.

Juliet looked down at the piece of paper in her hands. She had finished writing her tribute after a lot of crossing out and revision: *I met Luke on our first day at this school, four years ago —*

Tears stung her eyes, and she folded up the paper again. She would have to practice a lot more before she could stand up in front of everyone without losing it. She hadn't even known Luke that well, but she had liked the little she had seen of him. His sudden disappearance was so unnerving. And was he truly gone forever? He might have just run away for a while! But a lot of people seemed to act like he was dead. There was all that talk about "closure" — but how could you have closure when no one knew what had really happened to him? Something drifted into Juliet's mind — an image of ocean water closing over your head, swallowing you up as if you'd never existed at all. That's what had happened to Luke in a sense. If it wasn't for the posters, she doubted that anyone would remember him at all. Even Mark and Daniel, who seemed most affected by his disappearance, never talked about him.

And that was why Juliet had decided to speak at the service. She wasn't going to mention her doubts about his true fate — that would just be upsetting to everyone — but for the time being, she would do everything she could to keep his *memory* alive.

Juliet made a face as she and Christine stepped out of the hall into the cold, gray winter evening. It was November and nights were long and icy. But the usual abundance of after-school chatter hadn't changed as boys and girls milled around waiting for the bus or a ride home. Others took off on their bikes, their red taillights fading away into the gloom.

Juliet pulled her coat tightly around her. She and Christine lived on opposite sides of town, so they would head in different directions once they reached the front gate.

"Talk to you later?" Juliet said.

"Yeah." Christine shivered and tucked the ends of her scarf into her jacket. "Give me a call."

"Sure. Later." They set off, walking quickly with their heads down against the wind.

Juliet had been at the school for four years, since she was eleven, but it was the first time she had attempted this particular walk in the dark. Her family had moved over the summer. Daniel Gardner was her neighbor now; Luke's family lived three blocks away in a slightly older part of town. As she turned off the main road, Juliet noticed with a small prickle of discomfort just how much difference a lack of light made. All the usual landmarks — a bent lamppost, the heavily graffitied bus shelter — only became visible close up. Everything seemed to take longer; all the distances seemed more drawn out.

This was the route Luke would have taken every day. And one day, he had set off, like her, into the darkness — and never been seen again.

"Oh, great," Juliet muttered. "I *so* needed to think about that."

She turned right toward the park. Usually, she walked straight through it. In the summer, there would be kids playing baseball or splashing one another by the fountain. Now, Juliet realized, the park didn't have any lights. The road that ran around it was brightly lit, but the large open stretch of grass and bushes in between looked like a gaping black hole. Juliet took one look and decided she would walk around the perimeter of the park. It would only add ten minutes to her journey.

Her heels clicked on the pavement and cars swished by on the road, little islands of warmth in the dusk. *Maybe I should start bringing my bike to school*, she thought. *I'd put on the lights, stick to the main roads, and still get home in half the time.*

She came to Market Street on the far side of the park. It wasn't much more than a narrow alley opposite the park's north entrance, leading to the stores and businesses in the center of town. Juliet peered unhappily down the alleyway. It was the only way to get through without adding another twenty minutes to her journey. At the other end, she could see the center of town, brightly lit and busy with people and buses. It wasn't far — just a minute away at a brisk pace. After that, she would be on the main road, with streetlights all the way to her front door. She started to walk.

The darkness seemed to swallow her up in just a few paces. Once her eyes adjusted, she could see details of the buildings on either side. The walls and doorways were pale, the windows into them black voids. Nearly all the buildings on this street had been vacant for some time now.

Juliet approached the old butcher's shop and shuddered. Huge metal doors had been nailed across the entrance to discourage trespassers, and a large CONDEMNED notice was plastered across them. She could just make out the dark red paintwork and crumbling signs. The windows were veiled in dirt and cobwebs, and the shadows seem to cluster more thickly on the pavement outside.

To Juliet's surprise, there was a figure ahead, standing on tiptoes to peer into one of the grimy windows. Even though the light was very dim, Juliet recognized the tall, lanky frame and the mop of hair with low-hanging bangs. It was Daniel.

She called out into the darkness. "Daniel? It's me — Juliet."

Daniel spun around, looking startled. "I was . . . uh . . . checking for burglars," he stammered. "My dad owns this store. . . ."

"Burglars?" Juliet couldn't imagine anyone breaking into a place so cold and empty inside. "It doesn't look like anyone's been here, does it? It looks all locked up."

"Yeah . . . well . . ."

For a moment she thought their eyes might have met, but it was impossible to tell in the gloom. Then he brushed past her and headed back the way she had come, toward the park.

Juliet stood for a moment, watching his long-limbed silhouette trot into the light at the far end of the street. When his footsteps faded away, the street became abruptly quiet and cold again, its silence pressing down like an unwelcome fog. Suddenly, Juliet felt like an intruder — a warm, live human in this cold, dead place. As she started to walk toward the center of town, a shrill tune shattered the silence like ice.

Juliet jumped, then smiled, telling herself she'd let herself get spooked by the shadows. She fumbled to get her cell phone out of her bag as she walked quickly toward the bright lights. The little screen had lit up with an envelope icon and the words *1 message received*.

She selected the READ command and stared at the SENDER line. It wasn't from a number she recognized.

help me

Juliet scrolled down, but that was all there was.

Why would a stranger be asking for her help? "Help me" . . . do what?

Juliet selected REPLY.

who r u? wots wrong?

She paused as she was about to hit SEND. Maybe it was a marketing scam. If she replied to this number, she might be bombarded with texts about luxury vacations or credit card offers or get-rich-quick schemes.

Or maybe it was someone who really needed help. So she pressed SEND, just as she emerged into the busy, brightly lit center of town.

The final stretch home was uphill, to where the new housing development sat in what had once been fields overlooking the town. Juliet's phone chimed again as she reached her front door. The uphill slog had warmed her up, but she was looking forward to getting indoors and shutting out the cold, damp evening.

It was another text message.

Juliet clumsily turned the phone over in her gloved hands. The moment she stopped moving, a gust of frozen wind sliced right through her, doing nothing to improve her mood.

The message was from the same number.

im freezin

"Yeah, you and me both," she muttered. Clearly she

had a prankster on her hands — some idiot who had gotten hold of her number and decided to have some fun. She dropped the phone back into her pocket and pushed open her front door.

"Hey, wasn't it about this time last year that your classmate disappeared?" Juliet's father, never one to be up-to-the-minute, threw in the comment as the family were finishing dinner.

Juliet sighed. "Yes, Dad," she said. She had lost count of the times she had told him about the memorial service. It wasn't worth reminding him now.

"Must be hard for his parents," he remarked, picking up the newspaper.

Juliet rolled her eyes, but her mother thought it was a good time to contribute to the conversation.

"You remember, Alan," she said to Juliet's dad. "The school's having that service in a couple of days. Juliet's giving a speech."

"A reading, Mom," Juliet corrected her.

"Really?" Her father looked at her over the paper. "What about?"

"About Luke," she muttered.

"Luke?"

"The boy who vanished!" Juliet just controlled her temper as she scraped up her last spoonful of ice cream.

"Maybe we should run through whatever it is you're reading," her dad continued. "You do tend to swallow your consonants."

"Dad, I spent all afternoon rehearsing! I don't need to go through it again!"

Her dad narrowed his eyes at her. "There's no need to shout, young lady. Everyone needs to practice."

"Leave the poor girl alone, Alan," Juliet's mom said. "She's bound to get upset about this memorial service."

"That doesn't excuse bad manners," he said. "This boy Luke — was he your boyfriend?"

"Alan, I think Juliet would have told us!" her mother exclaimed. She looked sideways at her. "Wouldn't you? He *wasn't* your boyfriend, was he?"

"Mom, I hardly knew him," Juliet muttered.

"Fair enough, dear. But I'm very happy to hear from Christine that the two of you are making evening plans with Daniel and Mark. It will do you all good."

"What?" Juliet said. This was the first she had heard of it! She would throttle Christine and smile while she did it.

"Well, I talked to Christine earlier and . . . oh, sorry, was I not supposed to know?" Her mother winked. "Is it a *secret?"*

Juliet buried her face in her hands and left the table to go upstairs as soon as she could without being snapped at.

"Practice that speech!" her father called after her.

Later that night, Juliet lay in bed with the light out, looking up at the ceiling. She had spent the evening staring at her math homework. Usually it all made sense — in fact math was one of her strongest subjects — but tonight the equations had just been so many squiggles on the paper. Her mind was running in too many different directions to think about the value of x or y. Luke, death, her annoying dad . . .

And thanks to her best friend, her mom was convinced she had a new boyfriend.

"God, you're going to get it, Christine," she mumbled,

just as her cell phone went off again. She fumbled around on her bedside table as the display on her phone lit up, casting a ghostly glow around the room.

It was the same number as before.

i cant get out

Juliet groaned. Who was this jerk?

She stopped for a second.

Suppose someone really did need her help? OK, it was someone who only bothered to send texts every few hours, so he or she couldn't be in *that* much trouble — whatever the problem was, it was obviously taking its time to reach a critical moment — but even so . . .

Juliet sat up in bed. She would respond right now and find out. If this person really was in trouble, she would see what she could do. And if it was just someone messing around, this idiot would be *very* sorry.

Juliet selected CALL BACK and held the phone to her ear. While the call connected, there was nothing but the sound of her own heartbeat echoing off the phone and back into her head.

Suddenly, the phone blasted a shrill buzzing noise

into her ear. A polite voice said: *"Sorry, the number you have dialed is either disconnected or no longer in service. Please hang up and try again."*

"What do you mean?" Juliet said out loud, though she knew it was only a recording. "That's impossible!" She received the message only moments ago. How could she be getting messages from a number that didn't exist?

She knew how you could do that with e-mail — fake the headers in a message so that it appeared to come from somewhere else. But she hadn't heard of it being done with a text.

On the bright side, if someone was doing it deliberately, at least that meant the person couldn't be in any trouble. Someone was obviously pulling a prank on her, and she wasn't going to give anybody the satisfaction of getting all worked up about it. She pressed the OFF key with her thumb and held it down until the phone went dead.

Juliet woke up feeling extremely well rested, despite dreaming about equations. The other things that had been bothering her the night before seemed very distant. She felt for the light switch and scrunched up her eyes before turning it on.

Her phone lay where she had left it on her bedside table, its blank gray screen staring up. She switched it back on. While the screen went through its wake-up process, she put it down again and headed for the bathroom.

The message tune played before she reached the door.

Juliet stopped. She turned and looked at the phone. Uncertainty tugged at the back of her mind. Was it another one of those dumb messages? She turned around and crossed the room in two steps. Snatching up the phone, she checked the message screen. She was going to give this creep *such* a . . .

The message was from Christine. It had been sent last night, after Juliet had turned off her phone.

"Oh — Christine!" Juliet breathed in relief.

hi j! wanna come to high st aftr school 2 hit the stores?

Shopping with Christine suddenly seemed like the

best idea ever. It would take her mind off the idiot who kept texting her. Juliet grinned as she sent back:

Sure! cu l8r

The phone beeped again almost immediately, and she smiled as she glanced down at the screen. Christine was obviously in need of some serious retail therapy! Then she read:

im scared

On her way to school that morning, Juliet stomped down the hill in a foul mood. She now had four messages on her phone from a number that didn't exist, and whoever was at the other end either had a sick sense of humor or needed her help badly.

The weather did nothing for her mood. It was warmer than yesterday, but made up for that with a very fine drizzle. The water seemed to hang in the air, and you only realized it was there after it had already soaked you. By the time Juliet reached the bottom of the hill, she knew she was going to arrive at school dripping wet.

But, slowly, something penetrated her bad temper — an awareness that she was not alone. She was being followed by a car — a car that was slowly pursuing her down the street and matching her exact same pace.

She was in no mood for this at all. Deciding that she probably wasn't about to be abducted in broad daylight, she stopped with her hands on her hips and glared right into the windshield. The vehicle was a brand-new, metallic blue sports car, its windows misted with fine drops of water.

The driver's window slid down, and a young man peered out. "Hey, Julie!"

Juliet relaxed at once. "Dave!" She looked quickly from left to right, then darted across the street.

Dave was her cousin. He was only a few years older than her, close enough to be more like her big brother, especially since she didn't have any real brothers or sisters.

"Need a lift to school?" Dave offered.

Juliet grinned. "Sure!"

She ran around to the passenger door and climbed

in. Inside it was warm and dry. It smelled fresh and leathery — like so many new cars do.

"Very nice," she said approvingly as she admired the spotless interior. "How long have you had it?"

"Picked it up on Friday," Dave said proudly. "I've got a promotion coming up so I thought I'd celebrate."

"That's great," she said. "They must really like you down at the station!" Dave was a police officer. He was wearing part of his uniform now — he had on his own winter jacket, but underneath she could see a crisp, white shirt collar, a dark blue tie, and matching trousers.

Maybe my entire family isn't useless, Juliet thought. "Dave," she began slowly, "can I ask you something?"

Dave listened carefully as she told him about the messages. When she had finished, his face was stern. "Julie, if you're being harassed, then you have to report it! Tell the phone company. They can cut the guy off if they have to."

"But the number doesn't exist!" she reminded him.

"It exists, or it wouldn't be calling you. It's called spoofing, Jules — it's perfectly possible to disguise the identity of a cell phone. It just takes a bit of extra know-how. I'd be surprised if the company can't track it."

Juliet paused, turning her phone over in her hands. She wanted to ask Dave a really big favor. "Could *you* track it? I mean, if I didn't make this a formal report — could you do it, just between the two of us?"

Dave looked at her for a moment, then turned back to the road. "Well, I could," he said. "But we get into all kinds of trouble if we use police resources for our own purposes. Unless you actually want to report this guy, Julie, it's not police business."

"But I don't want to report him — whoever it is," Juliet said helplessly. "That's why I'm asking you like this. I'm afraid of overreacting. If it's a sick stalker then, yeah, sure, I'd want to report him; if it's just some dumb kid at school who thinks he's funny, he wouldn't be worth making a fuss about. And if it's someone in trouble, well, I want to help him. But I don't know which it is! And I won't know unless I know where the number is coming from." She broke off in confusion.

They had reached the school, and Dave pulled over. "Can I see these messages, Julie?"

She handed him her phone and watched him scroll through the texts. He raised his eyebrows as he read each one under his breath.

Suddenly, Juliet gasped and gripped the edge of her seat. A vision had hit her, an absolute certainty about the stranger at the other end of the line. It was someone alone, cold, and scared. And in the dark. A small, dark, closed space. He was hardly able to breathe. . . .

Juliet bit her lip. Where had all that come from? There was no way she could know all that from just a few dumb texts. It was just someone messing around, right?

Dave was looking at her, concerned. "It's really getting to you, isn't it?" he said softly. She nodded, not trusting herself to speak. He sighed and handed the phone back.

"Write down the number," he said, "and I'll see what I can do."

Juliet felt slightly better as she walked onto the school grounds. Maybe by the end of the day, Dave would have told her who had made the calls, and she'd be able to confront this deviant. She couldn't wait to see the look on the person's face.

Christine ambushed her just inside the gate. "Julie! Julie! It's *so* cool!" Juliet let herself be dragged over to the edge of the playground. Christine's eyes were shining, and there were spots of bright color on her cheeks.

"Mark said he'd go out with me! With *me*! And he's going to meet us on High Street this afternoon."

"Us?" Juliet echoed.

"Of course, us! You said you'd come, remember?"

Juliet had completely forgotten about agreeing to go shopping after school. Talking to Dave — and worrying about the stranger — had driven it out of her mind, even though she had really liked the idea when Christine first texted it. But Christine and Mark mooning over each other was the last thing she wanted. She wondered if she'd be able to find an excuse to get out of it before the end of the day — maybe Dave calling her with the stalker's identity.

"Sure," she replied.

The day dragged by, and Juliet's mood dragged with it. During lunch, her phone went off — but this time it was the usual ring tone. Someone was calling her, not texting, but she wasn't reassured when she looked at the screen and saw *Number withheld*.

"Hey, you going to answer that?" Christine asked,

and Juliet realized she had been standing with the phone in her hand, staring at it.

"Um, yeah, of course," she said. She pressed the green TALK key and carefully held it to her ear. "H-hello?"

"You sound totally spooked," said a man's voice. "Are you OK?"

Juliet exhaled in relief. "Hi, Dave. Yeah, I . . ." She wasn't sure what to say.

"Julie, I did some finding out about that, uh, thing you asked me to find out," he said.

Juliet's heart started to pound, and her fingers felt slippery against the phone. "Yes?"

Dave sighed. "Your spoofer is better than I thought. He's using a number that's been out of use for a year. It was last used one year ago tomorrow, in fact."

"By whom?" Juliet wanted to know.

"Sorry, Julie, that's personal information and I really can't hand it out. Look, take this to the phone company. That's the best thing you can do. Bye."

Juliet stared at the phone in frustration as the line disconnected. It sounded like Dave was convinced this was the work of a prankster using a dead number.

But what was the point of this prank? If someone was trying to freak her out, wouldn't it be better to call her? Maybe breathe heavily, try to get her to say something? Wouldn't this person want to hear how she sounded?

"OK," she murmured. She was going to get to the bottom of this. The surest way to become spooked was to *let* herself become spooked. But she could fight back instead. Confront him — whoever he was. Or she.

She selected the last message received, then thumbed *Reply* and sent back:

> *i dont know who u r but i cant help if u dont tell me wots going on*

The envelope icon spun around on the screen and the display read *Message delivered*. Almost immediately it switched to *Message received*, and the phone buzzed in her hand.

Juliet blinked in surprise and selected the new message.

> *im ya friend i need u*

Juliet almost dropped the phone. No way, *no way* could someone have had time to tap in a reply to her text. No way!

But someone had.

The stores were busy and lit with garish lights. It was mid-November, and the town was already bulldozing toward Christmas with decoration-overload and a constant background of cheesy Christmas songs. There were three levels inside the main shopping center and Christine and Juliet headed straight for the second floor, where all the best clothing stores were.

"So . . . ," Juliet said as they rode up the escalator.

Christine applied a dab of lip balm. The fake strawberry scent made Juliet feel a little sick. "Hmmm?"

"Um, what would you do if you had, um, a stalker?"

Christine twisted the lip balm back into its tube and dropped it into her handbag. "I don't know. Depends who, I suppose."

"Suppose you didn't know? Suppose he just had your phone number and kept sending you weird messages?"

Christine grinned. "That would be even cooler! I

could pretend I knew who it was and let my imagination run wild."

Juliet suspected Christine wasn't the right person to expect any sympathy from, especially when it felt weird telling her about the messages in the first place. "But —" she began.

"Look!" Christine gasped. They had reached the top of the elevator. Christine clutched Juliet's arm and dragged her in through the door of the nearest store. "You've got to help me," she insisted. "There are these two designer shirts, and they are both *so* cool, but I need to know which one Mark will like most. . . . Wait there."

She dropped Juliet's arm and vanished between the racks of clothes, leaving Juliet to fume silently. Weren't friends meant to talk to each other? How could you when one of them wouldn't listen to anything important?

She took out her phone and gazed at it as if it held the secret of the mysterious caller, and all she had to do was stare until it revealed his identity. She scrolled idly through the messages, until the last one appeared on the screen. . . .

Suddenly, the phone was snatched out of her hand.

"Julie! Really!" Christine was back — how long had she been there? — clutching a pair of shirts on hangers. "Pay attention, please! This is so much more important than . . ." She glanced at the message and her eyes nearly spun in circles.

"Oh, my God! Oh, my *God!*" For a moment, Juliet thought her friend was getting freaked out by the creepy messages — and oddly, this made her feel better. Maybe she wasn't overreacting after all.

But then Christine dropped her voice and looked from side to side, as if checking for dangerous spies. "So this is what you meant about text messages! You've got a *boyfriend!* Why didn't you tell me?"

Juliet snatched back the phone. "I do not have a boyfriend!" she hissed. "I don't know who it is. Someone's been sending me all these anonymous texts and —"

Christine drew in her breath sharply. Her hand flew to her mouth, smudging her carefully applied lip balm. "Wait, Julie! I know exactly who it is!"

"Who?" Juliet was ready to listen to any theory.

"It's *Daniel!* Come on, you know it makes sense! We're best friends, aren't we? And Mark and Daniel are best friends, so of course he wants to go out with you! He's trying to get a date!"

"By stalking me anonymously?" Juliet muttered, but Christine wasn't listening.

"Oh, Julie, the four of us together! This is so *fantastic!*" She pulled Juliet into a hug. "Look, let's forget these stupid shirts. Let's go and meet Mark right now. I told him you'd be here this afternoon. I'll bet you anything Daniel's with him."

Juliet doubted it, but she let Christine pull her out of the store. She couldn't recall Daniel ever showing the slightest sign of interest in her. If he *was* trying to ask her out . . . well, she had to admit that, yes, the four of them together did have a nice sound to it. Daniel had quite a nice smile, the few times he bothered to show it. It was kind of a shy smile, as though he was laughing at a private joke and he'd like to share it with you.

And if Daniel *was* sending the messages — well, that would be about a billion times less scary, because she would have no difficulty confronting him about it. She could make a joke out of it, tell him there were much better ways to get her attention, like inviting her to a movie or skipping gym class on a Friday afternoon to hang out.

But she didn't think it was him, and not just because Christine's logic was based more on hope than fact. Daniel had looked right through her when they had passed outside the butcher's shop — in fact, hadn't he been running away from her when the first text arrived a few seconds later? He hadn't shown the slightest sign of being interested in her then, and he couldn't have sent a text while he was bolting down the alley toward the park. No, Juliet didn't believe Daniel was the one.

Whoever was texting her was still out there — but where?

One of Christine's predictions turned out to be true, however: Daniel was with Mark when they met up. The boys had already staked out a table at The Coffee Place. Mark stood up as soon as he saw them coming.

"Hey, Christine," he said with a smile. There was a warmth there that was at odds with Juliet's impression of him so far — withdrawn and reserved, and impatient with people he didn't know very well. Maybe he really did care for Christine, and maybe she really was help-ing him get over the Luke thing. If so, Juliet was glad.

"Hey, Mark," Christine gasped, and she clutched at Juliet's arm for a moment. Juliet tried not to wince.

Daniel followed Mark's lead more slowly, his gan-gly frame unfolding from his chair. He looked at Juliet, and she was *almost* certain Christine was wrong about his feelings. Daniel's bangs hid his eyes, and it was hard to tell what he was thinking, but the set of his mouth didn't show much enthusiasm.

"Hi, Juliet," he said flatly.

"Hi," she replied, equally flatly.

If he was going to be *that* uninterested, she realized, he probably wasn't going to offer drinks, and she was thirsty.

"May we get you something?" she said pointedly.

He shrugged. "Sure. Coke."

"Yeah, that would be good," Mark added.

"OK," Christine said. She looked deliriously happy at the privilege of getting a drink for her boyfriend. "Ice? Slice of lemon?"

Slice of lemon? In this place? Not very likely. "Come

on, Christine, we haven't got all day," Juliet muttered, dragging her over to the counter.

The girl behind the counter seemed determined to break records for slow service. It would have been just as quick to wait for her to grow a couple of lemon trees out back. Christine took the first two Cokes over to the table, and Juliet had to wait a couple more minutes for the next two. When she returned to the others, her heart plummeted as she heard what Christine was chatting about.

". . . some secret admirer, *texting* her all the time . . ."

The way Christine said it, and the way she was looking at Daniel out of the corner of her eye, showed exactly who she thought was sending the messages. Daniel just looked bored.

"It's really not a big deal. . . ." Juliet began.

"Not a big deal?" Christine protested. "Come on!"

Before Juliet could stop her, Christine yanked the phone from Juliet's bag, called up the message menu, and thrust the tiny screen into Daniel's face. Juliet's hands were full of Coke glasses, and she could only watch helplessly in dismay.

"So what do you make of that, Daniel?" Christine demanded.

Daniel took the phone and looked at the screen.

His face went white, and he slammed the phone down on the table as if it had burned his hands.

"Got a problem, Danny?" Mark said. He picked up the phone and looked casually at the screen. "Ah, it's nothing. Just some stupid marketing trick. They send stuff like this all the time, then charge you a fortune for replying. Forget it, Juliet. I've heard there are phones now that can block numbers you don't want calling you Maybe you should get one? What do you think, Dan?" He looked hard at his friend, and Daniel flushed.

"Uh, yeah," he said. "Good idea."

"Yeah," Juliet muttered. "Maybe." She remembered she had thought it might be a marketing hoax, the very first time she got a message. But since then, she had had that talk with Dave and learned about the old number. Surely, a marketing company would use a new number?

Daniel twitched back his sleeve and looked at his

watch. "Hey, I've, uh, gotta go," he said. "Got . . . uh . . . something." He pushed back his chair and smiled weakly at Juliet. "Sorry."

Mark frowned. "I thought we were going to see a movie?"

"Yeah, well, you know . . ." Daniel said vaguely. He was already backing away. As soon as he reached the door of the café, he turned and vanished into the crowds of shoppers.

Christine turned to Juliet, her eyes round with distress. "Oh, Julie, I'm so sorry! I didn't think he'd stand you up like that. That guy is such an idiot. . . ."

"Stand you up?" said Mark. "Has Dan asked you out or something?"

"Oh, come on," Christine said before Juliet could reply. "You just have to look at him. . . ."

"It's nothing," Juliet put in. "Really, it's nothing."

"Yeah, well, fancy technology always does freak Gardner out," Mark said, waving Juliet's phone. "This must have scared him away. Dan likes to live in the stone ages. He doesn't even have one of these."

"*What?*" Christine couldn't have sounded more

shocked if she had just learned Daniel lived in a cardboard box. "He doesn't have a cell phone!"

Juliet stared at Mark, gripping the edge of the table. "Are you sure about that? That he doesn't have a phone, I mean?"

"Nah, he can't stand them," Mark said casually. He sipped his Coke. "It really ticks me off when we're trying to plan football practice."

Juliet's mind was reeling. Even though she had been fairly sure it wasn't Daniel sending her the messages, the fact that he didn't have a cell phone meant it definitely wasn't. And right now, she wasn't sure how she felt about that. The idea of a truly anonymous stalker suddenly seemed even more threatening than before, and she wanted to get out of the stuffy café and find somewhere quieter to think. "Can I have my phone back, Mark?" she asked.

"Hmm?" Mark realized he was still holding her phone. "Oh, yeah, sure. Sorry."

He handed it back, and Juliet shoved it into her bag. Then she pushed back her chair and practically ran out of the café, trying to forget that *anyone* could be sending the text messages — maybe even someone in the shopping center, someone watching her right now, waiting for her to be alone. . . .

The murmur of the packed auditorium came through the thick stage curtains. Miss Worth was in organizing overdrive, her glasses shoved into her wiry hair as she coordinated Juliet and Christine and Mark and Daniel and everyone else who would be taking part in the memorial service. Today was The Day — exactly 365 days after Luke Benton's disappearance.

Juliet ran through her lines under her breath one more time. Christine had said she would help Juliet practice . . . but of course, Christine was on the other side of the stage with Mark. She looked completely out of place alongside the entire football team.

On an impulse, Juliet pulled her phone from her pocket. She opened up a blank message and texted: *hey, rmbr me?* She selected Christine's number and pressed SEND.

The phone vibrated in her hand — Miss Worth had told everyone to turn their phones off, and Juliet had compromised by setting it to silent mode. She frowned at the screen. The dialogue box read *Unable to send message* and showed a bulging envelope icon. She groaned. This happened when the in-box and out-box filled up with stored messages. It meant she would have to go through all her old text messages and decide which ones to delete. She knew she could just select DELETE ALL and empty her in-box entirely — but some of the old messages had sentimental value and she wanted to keep them a little longer.

There were still several minutes before the start of the memorial service. Juliet ducked her head and started to delete the routine messages — arranging with Christine to meet up after school, sharing gossip, checking on homework. That stuff was easy. But then she came to the five anonymous messages and realized she wasn't sure if she wanted to keep them or not. She moved the cursor idly up and down the list, looking at the brief, almost meaningless words, and the dates and times each message had been sent.

Then something odd struck her. She knew the most recent message had come in yesterday, and the first had arrived two days ago. But all the messages appeared to have been sent on the same day. And it was *today's* date.

For a moment, she wondered if something was wrong with her phone's memory card. She scrolled down to a different message, the one Christine had sent her about going shopping. No, that had the right date attached to it, two days ago. Juliet went back to the five anonymous messages.

There was something else odd about the dates. The day and the month were the same as today . . . but the year was different. The messages were dated this exact day one year ago.

Today, the anniversary of Luke Benton's disappearance, was also the anniversary of these texts being sent!

Even stranger, now that Juliet was in the frame of mind to notice things, were the *times* the messages seemed to have been written. They had been sent to her in reverse order, each one written a few minutes earlier than the one before. The last message she had received — *im ya friend* — was the first to be sent. If you put them into the right order, they read like this:

im ya friend i need u
im scared
i cant get out
im freezin
help me

Juliet felt icy droplets trickle down her spine. She shivered, even though it was hot and stuffy behind the curtains. She stared at the tiny screen, trying to make some sense — any sense — out of what was there. Then she almost dropped the phone when it suddenly started vibrating like an insect in her palm. She checked the screen and bit back a sob. Another message . . .

"Oh, no," she whispered. "Oh, no, oh, please, just go away."

It was from the same number as before, and it had been sent before any of the others.

the place is all locked up

"What place?" Juliet murmured. She shut her eyes, piecing together all the clues. It was freezing, it was locked up — she had that flash again of somewhere cold, dark, and airless, so hard to breathe. . . .

She shivered and thrust the phone back into her pocket. Where had all this stuff come from? This was really starting to get to her, worming its way into her thoughts. . . .

Something to do with the last message rang a

small bell in her mind. Something about being all locked up . . .

Market Street, she thought, and shuddered again. For a moment, it was as if she was back there on that cold, damp evening two nights ago. Halfway along Market Street, outside the deserted butcher's shop; Daniel looking through the filthy window, apparently checking for burglars.

"It looks all locked up," she had said.

It had only been a few moments after that when the first message came in.

"**H**ey, Julie, where are you going?"

Christine's voice was muffled by the damp evening mist, and Juliet pretended not to hear as she burst out of school. She had slipped away from the crowd as soon as the service was over, and now she stuffed her hands in her pockets and walked quickly down the street. For a moment, she felt guilty for avoiding Christine like this. But then she reminded herself that Christine just didn't — couldn't — understand how creeped out Juliet was, and it would take too long to explain why. This was something Juliet had to do on her own.

She continued walking into the darkness.

A cold wind was blowing down Market Street, and the dank gloom of the narrow lane only made it seem colder, even more like a scene from an old black-and-white movie.

The butcher's shop had been little more than a black shape the last time Juliet saw it, its windows dark holes into the unknown. Now that she could see it more clearly, in the reddening twilight, it looked even more menacing. It was square and blocky and ugly. Its paint seemed deliberately tattered, as if it had never appeared new, even when it was first painted. It was like the disrespectful kid in school who sits through class with his feet up on the desk.

Juliet didn't jump when her phone shattered the silence with its message tone. She had almost expected another clue. She checked what had come in.

i fink they all went home

Juliet shuddered. Whoever had sent this was all alone — just like she was now.

"I wish I was home, too," she muttered.

She pressed her face to the window. The grimy glass reflected her own face back at her — a pale pinkish smudge against the gray — and she could see nothing except for a few hard-edged shapes inside. The bottom of the pane was smeared with hand marks; she wondered if they belonged to Daniel, from when he had been peering in. Juliet wondered why his dad hadn't invested in proper security if he was so concerned about burglars.

She stepped back from the store and gazed up at its decaying front.

"So what exactly am I doing here?" she wondered out loud. Surely it was just a coincidence that this was where she'd received the first anonymous text, right?

"Ah, forget it," she muttered. "Get a grip, Julie."

She turned to go, and her phone sounded.

Juliet stopped dead. What were the chances, she wondered hopefully, that Christine was texting her to say she had split up with Mark?

Very faint, she knew as she pulled out the phone. Very faint indeed.

It wasn't Christine; it was the year-old number.

they locked me in

Juliet's breath caught in her throat. Locked in! It doubled the horror of the vision she'd had before. If she'd thought about it at all, she'd somehow assumed the person had ended up in the freezing, dark, airless room by accident. That was bad enough.

Had they been locked in *deliberately?*

Juliet scanned the sheets of metal nailed over the front of the shop. Not even a door handle showed. She looked around and saw the dark slit of a narrow passageway running between this store and the next one. The front door was boarded up, but there had to be a back one.

i cant get out

Juliet inched down the passageway, turning sideways when her feet squelched in something she didn't want to inspect too closely. Her shins connected hard with what felt like a garbage pail and she cursed under her breath, then louder when she realized there was no one to hear her. At last, the walls of the passageway fell away on either side, and she stumbled into the yard at the back of the store.

It was enclosed by high brick walls, topped with rusty barbed wire and broken glass. From the piles of trash shoved against the edges, with shadows that seemed to shift and blur in the gloom, it looked like the whole street used this place as a garbage dump. But sure enough, there was a door into the back of the old butcher's shop, and it didn't seem to have been boarded up.

Juliet put her hand on the handle and pushed, then shook it. Not boarded, but still locked fast with a new and strong-looking padlock just above the handle. She could also see some evidence of a conventional dead bolt. There was a window in the top half of the door, with a blind pulled down inside to hide the store from view. The window was covered by a metal grille attached to the outside, reddish with rust and twisting away from the wooden frame at one corner.

im ya friend i need u

Juliet stepped back, and her foot knocked into something that made a metallic clink. She had dislodged a small heap of metal pipes, stacked against a battered china sink. She bent down and wrapped her hands around a cold, heavy length of pipe. She slid one end into the loop of the padlock and pushed down as hard as she could. The clasp bent slowly at first, then broke open with a jerk.

That leaves the dead bolt, Juliet thought. She'd have to smash the window and reach in to open it from the inside. She threaded her fingers into the grille and tugged. She felt something shift, but after that the grille held fast. She picked up the pipe again and jammed it carefully between the door and the grille. The grille lifted away from the woodwork, its screws tearing free with a splintering crack. It came apart more quickly than Juliet was expecting, and her knuckles banged into the rough brick wall. She examined her hand — only a minor scrape. Now she just had to break the window, and she'd be able to get in.

She swung the pipe and tried not to feel too satisfied when the glass shattered. She reached gingerly in through the hole, being careful not to cut herself on the jagged glass stuck in the frame. Something cold and damp brushed against her fingers and she almost screamed, until she realized it was only the shade inside the door.

i fink they all went home

Her fingers found the latch of the dead bolt, though she had to stand at an odd, shoulder-straining angle to reach it. She took a firm grip and twisted. The latch gave way with a rusty snap. She put her shoulder against the frame and pushed. It slowly, grudgingly swung open. Just as slowly, Juliet sidled into the cold, dark building.

the place is all locked up

The store smelled of dust and mold. At first, all she could see were vague, squarish shapes and more pools of shadow. She instinctively fumbled for the light switch beside the door, and stifled a shriek as she thrust her fingers into a mass of cobwebs. She pulled her hand back and wiped it against her coat.

By now, her eyes were adjusting to the darkness. All the furniture, desks, anything that might have given a clue to what this room was before, had been taken away. The floor had a pattern of checked tiles, squares of dark and light gray that might have been white once upon a time.

Juliet took a step forward. She could hear something small moving around by her foot, something that skittered, something very much alive. She sprang backward and bumped into the wall, dislodging a small cloud of grit that fell into her hair. She brushed her hands frantically over her head while the small, dark shape — a mouse? a rat? — scuttled across the floor. It vanished into a hole in the wall on her right.

Juliet made herself take deep, steady breaths until she felt her pounding heart slow down. She looked around. There was a door straight in front of her that must lead to the main part of the store. Another door on her right stood half open, and she could just make out a flight of stairs beyond.

help me

There was a third door in the far left-hand corner of the room.

Is Anybody There?

It took a moment for Juliet to realize it was a door at all because it was taller and wider than the others. At first, she thought it was just a patch of wall that was painted differently. Now that her eyes had adjusted, she could make it out more clearly. It was darker than the wall next to it, and it gleamed metallically in the orange light that filtered from the boarded-up windows in the front of the store.

Juliet didn't know much about how a butcher's shop was run, but she knew there must have been a means to store everything. Something bigger than your typical fridge. This must have been the butcher's meat locker.

im freezin

She walked cautiously up to the door and ran her fingers over the brushed metal surface. There was a long, vertical handle at waist height. Knobs and dials were set into a panel on the wall next to it, which presumably had once set the temperature. They were all dead now, of course — the power long cut off.

they locked me in

The door was like the entrance to a bank vault. If any-one had been locked in somewhere in this building, this would be it. Any other room, you only had to knock the door down, or climb out of a window. But someone locked in here — what chance would they have to escape?

And did that mean Juliet really wanted to see what was on the other side?

She shuddered, but she took hold of the handle in both hands. She had come this far. She had to know.

She let go of the handle again. She *didn't* want to know. She wanted to go home, right now.

they locked me in

A sob exploded from deep within her as she stood still, trembling.

im scared

With a wordless shout of anger and fear, she gripped the lever and pulled. It didn't shift. She took hold of it again, braced her feet on the slippery floor, and heaved, grunting with the effort. Did it budge slightly? She braced again and threw herself backward, yanking on the lever as hard as she could.

Something clicked, and the door moved a couple of inches.

Juliet still needed both hands on the lever, but slowly the door opened. A blast of ancient air hit her directly in the face, followed immediately by a stench so horrible, so evil, that it made her gag. It was dead and rotting. It was everything that should not be.

they locked me in

Juliet staggered back with her sleeve over her mouth. Someone must have left some old meat hung up in there. It was the worst thing she had ever smelled.

She held her breath and took a step forward to peer into the storage room, but the space inside could have been as small as a phone box or as big as a football stadium for all she could see. The shadows inside seemed blacker and thicker than anywhere else, swallowing all the feeble light that penetrated the rest of the room. Juliet waited for her stomach to stop heaving, then pulled the door open as far as it would go to let the light in.

help me

The shadows slid back enough for Juliet to see that the room was a glistening steel-lined cube. The walls were sheer and smooth, and curved steel hooks dangled from racks on the ceiling. Sides of beef and bacon had once hung from them, but now they just swayed a little in the slight breeze that Juliet had caused. And the floor . . .

The floor was smooth and clean with white ceramic tiles. The stale, dusty orange light edged across it as the door opened, trickling over a pair of shoes lying in the far corner.

Sneakers — black with a silver trim.

Juliet pushed the door open the last few inches. The band of light shifted to reveal a wallet, a pair of sunglasses, and a cell phone lying next to the sneakers. Juliet forced herself to walk over to the small pile of abandoned belongings. She took a deep breath, then flipped open the wallet.

The first thing she saw was a school ID — with a familiar picture staring up at her.

Luke Benton.

He had been here. And something told her, it was the last place he had *ever* been. At least, alive.

Juliet dropped the wallet and picked up the phone. She was familiar with the model — she had the same one — and she knew how to turn it on, but nothing happened when she held down the POWER key. The battery had died long ago.

But there was one thing she could do. She quickly opened up the phone, pulled out the memory card, and swapped it with her own. She turned her phone on again, and the screen lit up with Luke's last messages.

There they were, in the out-box. All of them, in the order he had sent them — the reverse of the order she had received them.

they locked me in
i fink they all went home

None of them were listed as sent. Juliet scrolled

through the last message until she came to the message report. She flicked through the date and time of sending until she came to the final line: *Error: unable to send msg.*

"Oh, Luke," she murmured as her eyes filled with tears. "I can't believe they left you here. . . ." They must have gotten him out eventually, she thought. But by then, it must have been too late.

"Be quiet!"

"I'm trying!"

Juliet spun around. Someone else had entered the room at the back of the store; two voices, two sets of footsteps shuffling over the tiled floor. Instinct made Juliet move to one side, out of the cone of light that shone through the open door. She stood pressed against the wall. She couldn't see who was there, but that meant they couldn't see her, either.

"Look, we don't know someone's been in here. . . ."

"That door had been forced open!"

"OK, Danny, OK . . ."

Danny! Juliet shut her eyes and breathed out slowly in relief. She recognized the voices now. It was only

Daniel, still worried about burglars in his dad's store, and he had brought Mark along for support.

She opened her eyes, and saw the cone of light shrinking across the floor of the meat locker. She stepped away from the wall just in time to see the smooth steel door swinging shut.

Juliet screamed and ran toward it. It closed, and the light vanished at the same moment as she crashed against the metal.

"STOP! Open this door!" she shrieked. She dropped the phone and scrabbled blindly at the smooth, steel surface. *"Wait! Open the door! Daniel! Mark! Please! Open up!"*

It was so dark, she couldn't even tell if her eyes were open. She pressed against the door, not wanting to take her hands away because it was her only point of reference in the pure darkness. If she did take them away, she would be spinning in an endless black void.

Hadn't Mark and Daniel seen Luke's belongings through the open door? Obviously not. But they must have heard Juliet. She had screamed just before the door shut. Now that they knew she was here, they would open it immediately! Wouldn't they?

they locked me in

It took a second for the realization to sink in. Not *they shut me in.* Not *they accidentally closed the door on me.* Just *they locked me in . . .* and then, *i fink they all went home.*

"Oh, no," Juliet whispered. "Mark and Daniel!" She sank down to the floor with her back against the cold metal door.

    im scared
    i cant get out
    im freezin

Juliet didn't know how much time passed before she started thinking in a straight line again. She had to get out, and it was obvious that Mark and Daniel weren't coming back for her. She had dropped her phone — well, she had to find it again. Juliet got on to her knees and crawled forward, slowly moving her hands across the slippery ceramic tiles.

She felt her hand knock against something small and hard. It clattered across the floor, but she grabbed it before it could slip too far. Then, by feel, she pressed the MENU button.

The display and the keypad lit up in green, and she breathed a grateful sigh. She had light. She had a way of talking to the world.

im ya friend i need u

The damp, stinking air pressed around her. Juliet didn't know how much oxygen was in this steel crypt, but if she kept calm, it should last a while. Long enough for someone to come and get her. She called up the message menu, thumbed out the words *help me*, and selected Christine's number.

The whirling envelope appeared on screen, meaning that the message was being sent. Juliet slumped back against the wall with relief.

The phone beeped and she smiled in the dark, then checked to see what Christine had said.

It wasn't from Christine, and though she stared at the screen for a long time, the words just wouldn't sink in.

Error — unable to send msg

When she finally figured it out, she knew without a trace of uncertainty that Luke had had the same thought one year ago, when his desperate messages failed to arrive. She was entombed within four solid walls of metal. No phone signal would get through this. Her cell phone didn't have a chance.

Juliet screamed and screamed until her throat was raw.

She knew no one could hear her, but it didn't matter. She was beyond rational thinking. All she knew was that the darkness was closing in, and the cold was numbing her fingers and stealing her breath away.

She wouldn't be able to last very long in here. The only question was, which would disappear first: the oxygen, or her sanity? She almost hoped it was the latter. Perhaps she'd let the darkness take over as she calmly slipped away to some small, peaceful place in her mind. . . .

She slumped against the wall and closed her eyes, listening to the silence. Now that she'd stopped screaming, there was no sound except her rasping breaths. Soon they would stop, too, she realized, and the entire room would be silent.

Dead silent.

The thought made her want to scream again, but she didn't have the energy. Instead she just shook quietly, tears running down her face.

Then she heard it. A low, creaking sound. Juliet thought she was imagining it, until she realized that the darkness was lifting. She could see her hand in front of her face, then the smooth walls of the room. *Is this it?* she wondered dimly. *Does the end come so fast?*

And then her mind snapped back into place. The room was growing lighter because the door was slowly swinging open. She was free! Juliet sprung to her feet, eager to meet her rescuer. She stepped out of the meat locker and into the store, but the place was still dark and empty. There wasn't a soul. Or was there?

Juliet took one last look at the meat locker, her gaze stopping at the small pile of Luke's belongings. Somehow she knew who had opened the door.

She slipped out of the store, gulped down a deep breath of fresh air, and pulled out her phone. She dialed the number that had grown so familiar, that she now knew was *Luke's* number. And she typed in her message:

thank U

It was only a moment before the phone alerted her to an incoming message.

no prob. now RUN

Run? She looked up from the phone. Mark and Daniel were walking down the lane — straight toward her.

Juliet sprinted in the opposite direction, her lungs heaving as she pushed herself faster and faster. She could hear Mark and Daniel — the star athletes — racing behind her now, and she forced herself to speed up, even as her leg muscles screamed in pain.

She knew she must escape. Someone had to tell the authorities what had happened to Luke. She was determined to make sure the truth came out.

Juliet owed Luke that much.

She owed him everything.